# FAIRBANKS

D. G. WOODS

FAIRBANKS

D. G. Woods

Summary:

When a mysterious disaster strikes, a family of four in Fairbanks, Alaska must fight to survive as communication systems, transportation, and essential services disintegrate. With their world turned upside down, they're forced to make desperate choices and confront the harsh realities of their new existence.

Fairbanks is a haunting and intimate novella about human nature, fear, and survival, stripping away the comforts of modern life and leaving only the raw, primal struggle to stay alive—and to protect your family at all costs.

This is a work of fiction. While the story is set in a real city in Alaska and references actual places and Indigenous groups, the characters, events, and storyline are entirely fictional and not intended to represent real events or people.



Text copyright © 2025 by D. G. Woods

Cover design © 2025 by Holly Lowe of Hollowe Studios

Edited by Ayee Caparra, Moonlight Words Literary Services

All rights reserved.

Published in the United States of America by

Cabins Press LLC

ISBN-13: 979-8-9920445-1-5 (Paperback edition)

ISBN-13: 979-8-9920445-0-8 (Ebook edition)

First Edition: February 23, 2026

Printed in the United States of America

# CONTENT WARNINGS

This book contains mature themes that may be triggering for some readers. If you're concerned about specific triggers, please review the list below:

Racism, prejudice, xenophobia
Classism
Ableism
Societal collapse
Emotional abuse
Mentions of domestic abuse and violence
Mentions of child abuse
Death of a child
Alcohol and substance abuse

*For Wes*

The world has already ended.
You just haven't noticed yet.

# 1

# CLARA

The shelves were bare.

"No eggs? What the hell?" a woman muttered beside Clara.

Clara didn't respond. She tightened her jaw and pushed the cart forward. She hated when strangers commented as if they were speaking to her, as if the obvious needed to be pointed out aloud. She could see the empty shelves just fine. There was no need to announce it.

Back home she might have answered, might have shared a look or a joke. Here she had no patience for any of it. Everything felt different, from the climate to the people. She kept to herself now, careful and closed off, moving through the store as quickly as possible, trying to limit how much of the outside world could reach her.

Walking away, she glanced into the woman's overflowed cart, filled with dry grains sealed in thick plastic. Clara pressed her lips together. *That* she didn't understand. The way some people shopped, you'd think tomorrow was already in question. Folks here moved through the world differently. Where she came from there were oddballs, certainly, but this felt like something else entirely. A separate species. *Alaskans*.

The sudden egg shortage annoyed her. She'd checked both the East and West Freddy's and come up empty-handed. Eggs were a staple in their house. Cereal didn't count as a real meal, too much sugar and too little nutritional value, so Clara rotated between scrambled eggs with sausage and oatmeal. But oatmeal was universally hated. Caleb scrunched up his face every time a bowl of the gluey stuff was set in front of him, and after three mornings of it he refused to eat at all.

And still, the shelves stayed empty. For days now there hadn't been a single egg in the store. The woman's frustrated remark about the missing provisions grated on Clara, as if someone had spoken a dark thought she'd been trying not to name, and by saying it out loud made it real. She pushed the feeling aside. It was just eggs. An inconvenience. Probably another bird flu they weren't reporting yet.

There was no time to try another store. With a sigh, Clara grabbed two cartons of liquid egg product, hoping they'd pass for the scrambled dish and the kids wouldn't notice the difference. She added a box of Froot Loops too, just in case Caleb and Sophie threw a fit, and headed for the checkout.

Clara loaded the groceries into the trunk and sank into the driver's seat. For the first time that morning she could let go, if only for a moment, and reach for her phone to connect with her family—not the one she was responsible for, but the one where she could still be a daughter and a little sister. Yesterday she had sent her mother a photo of the kids in front of the TV, taken just before Caleb sighed and stomped out in protest. Sophie, however, stayed put, quietly smiling at the camera. Her mother usually replied within hours, sometimes minutes. Currently retired, she lived vicariously through her children and grandchildren, always on the phone with one of her two daughters. Yet an entire day had passed, and there were still no new notifications.

Only then did Clara notice the message hadn't gone through.

Tiny red letters marked it as failed. The service was terrible here in Fairbanks. Though David kept insisting it wasn't, that coverage was better than back home, and that the problem was probably Clara's phone. He never offered a solution, and eventually Clara stopped bringing it up. With a pang of annoyance—this time at David, even though he wasn't to blame for the poor signal—she sighed and tapped resend. The message stalled, then failed again.

She tried calling her mother. It didn't go through. She tried once more. Same result. Then she called David. This time the call connected, but he didn't answer, which made sense. He was at work.

Clara dropped the phone back into her purse and fumbled with her keys just as it started ringing. Of course *now* the stupid thing decided to function. She knocked the purse onto the car floor and swore through gritted teeth, something she'd definitely scold the kids for, before finally fishing the phone out again. David was calling her back.

"Hey, just checking if my phone's working," she said as a greeting, "I've been trying to reach Mom."

"What's wrong with your phone?" David's voice carried that familiar edge, one Clara had grown used to over the years, like she was just another nuisance in his day.

"I don't know. I just can't get through."

"I'm at work. What do you want me to do?"

Clara knew better than to call him during duty hours unless it was an emergency. With no one else to turn to, she'd tried anyway.

It had been over six months since the move to Fairbanks, and Clara still felt out of step with everyone around her At school the other moms had already carved out their circles, chatting over coffee and playdates, swapping advice as if she didn't exist. Besides, her daughter's constant colds and other medical issues made it even harder to focus on personal relationships. She didn't fit in, and part of her didn't want to. They were just so different from the people she'd known back home.

In Gastonia she'd had a tight circle of friends, but they'd faded little by little, and Clara found herself scrolling through Facebook updates, feeling like a ghost peeking into a world she no longer belonged to. She didn't blame her friends for not reaching out. Everyone was busy with work, kids, and life. She didn't want to bother them either.

These days her calls were mostly to her mother and sister. Outside her family Clara barely spoke to anyone, and her family consisted of the always annoyed and snappy David, her teenage son Caleb, who mostly communicated through grumpy humming and monosyllabic answers, and her daughter Sophie, quiet and sweet. Though talking to an eight-year-old, while pleasant, was a poor substitute for adult conversation. The isolation was starting to wear Clara down.

Her phone seemed to be working fine. The issue had to be on her mother's end. Clara could message her on Facebook, though her mom never used it. Years ago, Clara and her sister had helped her set up an account, and they doubted she had opened it since.

Clara started driving, hoping to be home by the time the bus dropped the kids off, and called her sister to make sure everything was okay. Anxiety gnawed at her from the inside. She needed to hear something simple, a reassurance that Mom was fine, that it was just her phone dying, or maybe she'd dropped it in the bathroom. Again. Something easy, reasonable. Something that would make Clara laugh with relief.

Leaving her family behind had been harder than she'd expected. Back in North Carolina she'd been the one who checked in on their mother, still adjusting to her new hip. Clara stopped by a couple of times a week to help with groceries, make dinner, or just sit and talk. Ashley was a lifeline, too, often babysitting when Clara needed a break. Clara returned the favor now and then, though hosting Ashley's three boys—ages seven, nine, and eleven—was never her favorite task. They were loud, always moving, always fighting. Clara loved them, but they'd exhausted her.

She often considered herself lucky to have had just one son, now seventeen, and then her daughter, her gentle girl. She loved Caleb, of course, as any mother would, but it was Sophie who held her heart in a way Clara couldn't admit out loud. Not even to herself.

The call to her sister also failed. It wasn't that Ashley didn't answer; the line simply wouldn't connect. Clara kept glancing at her phone while trying to focus on the road. Snow was falling thick and fast, reducing visibility with every passing minute. The car's heater blasted warm air. Clara still shivered. She hated the cold.

The roads, the failing signal, the isolation, it all chipped away at her. What had started as irritation thickened into something heavier, a mix of worry and frustration she could neither name nor act on. She tried to swallow it, the way she had for the past six months, but this time it settled in her chest and wouldn't move. Something was wrong.

Fairbanks didn't seem so bad in the summer. In contrast, winter came early and hard. The sun barely skimmed the horizon, as though it was too tired to rise. Even during the short days, the light wasn't the pretty, snow-globe kind. It was a cold, gray-blue twilight that made everything look washed out and sad.

Clara, born and raised in North Carolina, where winters were milder (still chilly, but not uncommon to have highs in the teens or twenties even in January), wasn't used to such extreme weather. On the most glacial mornings, she'd walk into the living room to find the couch cover literally frozen to the wall, fused by a thick line of white rime that had crept in through the siding. The cold left her drained and gave her headaches, though she could push through. Her daughter, however, was weaker. The harsh climate was cruel to Sophie's fragile build and asthma, and as soon as the temperature dropped she began to fall ill.

Back home, she sometimes left for school without her inhaler, which Clara always scolded her for. Here Sophie couldn't go anywhere without it. Even then, it didn't help. Her colds would drag on, creeping into bronchitis. She'd miss school, stay home, and spend her evenings connected to a nebulizer.

The sight of her little girl pale and coughing, with a mask over her tiny face, carved into Clara like a blade. But there was nothing to be done. David had said even this was better than the alternative: losing their house and becoming dependent on her mother. And sure, they had their disagreements with her mom, so at first she'd sided with her husband. Now, she couldn't help but feel they'd made a terrible mistake.

Before they came to Alaska, she'd had hardly any time to research the place. David handled everything: finding the house, arranging the relocation, even selling their old home without losing money, while she just sat numb, watching life rearrange itself without her. The next thing she knew, they'd been landing in Fairbanks.

At home—their new home, the modest three-bedroom-one-bathroom they rented—she unpacked the groceries, waited for the children to return, and made them a snack. Caleb, however, refused in his usual grumpy mumbling manner.

"I'm going out," he said, offering nothing more.

Clara didn't press. He was old enough to be on his own for a few hours, and Fairbanks seemed safe enough. He was going to see his girlfriend, Naya, a girl with long black hair and a serious, unsmiling face. That unsettled Clara. She felt the same worries every mother does when her teenage son experiences his first romance. There was the obvious: teenage pregnancy, a future derailed, and the trouble Naya might drag him into—drugs, alcohol, or other risky, illegal activities. She didn't know how to voice any of this to Caleb, so she let it play out, hoping somehow it would be okay.

If anyone had adjusted quickly, it was Caleb. He was the same grumpy, withdrawn teenager he'd been in North Carolina, only here he had a girlfriend—a Native girl—and a small group of friends. He hadn't had any close friends back home, not since that terrible incident with his childhood friend. And though Clara was glad he was finally coming out of his shell, a part of her bristled. Couldn't he have picked a *normal* American girl instead?

David buried himself in work, and even Sophie made a few friends at school. But for a thirty-eight-year-old stay-at-home mother, there was nothing. No community and no belonging.

She exchanged polite words with the neighbors, a slightly younger childless couple, both in the military, yet friendliness was as far as it went.


"Couldn't reach Ashley either," Clara said at dinner.

"Hm?" David looked up, as if only just noticing her.

"My phone. The calls wouldn't connect."

"At all?"

"No." Her patience was thinning. She had already explained this to him earlier. Did he not remember? Or was he gaslighting her? He'd always acted this way with her. When her car wouldn't start, when there was a problem with the heat. Things he, as *the man of the house*, was supposed to fix. Instead he just ignored her. Then he acted like he'd never heard of the matter whenever she brought it up again.

She forced a deep breath, swallowing her growing anger, before saying, "It works locally. Just not outside."

"Maybe you need a new phone, Mommy," Sophie chimed in.

Clara gave her a small smile before turning back to David. "Could you look at it?"

He shrugged. "Sure."

She handed him the phone after dinner and went back to the kitchen. He put on his glasses and held the device at a shifting distance, moving it closer and farther as he searched for clarity. His eyesight had been failing for years. Clara didn't mind, but it reminded her she was getting older too.

David scrolled through her settings. He toggled flight mode, checked the data, and tried calling his own phone. It went through.

"Hm." He set both the phone and his glasses on the counter. "Try again."

Clara wiped her hands and picked up the phone, giving him a look that said, *Why couldn't you just do it yourself?* He never called her family, and they never reached out to him. The dislike was mutual.

Clara ringed her mother again. Two quick beeps, then the line dropped.

"You should call the phone company. I don't know what's wrong with that thing," David said, pushing back from the counter with a heavy sigh.

*An old man's sigh,* Clara thought, swallowing one of her own.

The next day, Clara stood by the window, looking out at the dull street under a heavy sky. The whole scene looked as if someone had turned the colors off, leaving only shades of gray. She peeled off the window and closed the blinds, keeping the grayness outside, and called the phone company. She explained her problem carefully, only to be met with a voice she could barely hear over the static and background chatter.

"Everything looks fine on our end, ma'am," the operator said.

"But I still cannot get through to anyone."

"Are other calls working?"

"Yes."

"Then it must be on the recipient's side. Possibly a temporary outage. Nothing we can fix here."

Clara thanked him and hung up unsatisfied. She tried her mother again. Then her sister. Nothing.

She switched to her messenger app. Her mother never used it, so she tried her sister. Same result. No connection. She sent them both short texts, asking for a call back as soon as possible.

After some hesitation, she dialed Melany's number. Melany had faded from her life the moment Clara moved away. *Ghosted* wasn't the right word; they'd simply lost the one thing holding their friendship together—the school their daughters had attended. Without that there was nothing left to talk about.

The call to Melany didn't connect either.

Clara opened her browser and typed *North Carolina cell service interruptions*. No results came up. In fact there were no fresh articles at all. The world was never that quiet, not with the twenty-four-hour news cycle.

She thought about calling David again, but remembered the clipped tone he'd used when she called his office yesterday. She set the phone face down on the table and pushed it away.

Then she got up and returned to the window, peering outside again to make sure she wasn't going mad and that things were still normal. Everything seemed ordinary: her neighbor clearing the driveway, a dog pawing at a frosted window, the steady quiet of the late afternoon. So why did it feel so wrong?

She pulled on her coat and stepped onto the porch.

"Hey Jessica!" she called, waving.

Her neighbor paused, leaning on her shovel. "Oh hey there!"

Clara didn't want to shout across the street. Hugging her

arms close, she crossed over. The cold bit through her coat, seeping under her clothes, making her skin prickle—she should have put on more layers. Trash cans stood in front of houses as though guarding them. Some overflowed with garbage, bags spilling out, turning them into odd, modern-art-like pieces Clara could never understand. The truck hadn't been through yet.

"Has something happened?" Jessica asked.

"I don't know. I can't get through to my family in North Carolina. Have you had any trouble with service or is it just me?"

Jessica shrugged. "Not that I've noticed."

"Well." Clara forced a small smile, unsure what else to say. "Thanks anyway."

"Anytime." Jessica returned to her shoveling and a shivering Clara hurried back across the road, then forced herself to turn back, remembering something.

"Oh one more thing. Could I use your phone? I can't get through to my mom. I just want to make sure she's okay."

"Sure."

It took Clara three attempts to type in her mother's number with frozen fingers. When she pressed *call* cautious hope sparked in her chest. If only she could hear her mom's voice, she'd feel better immediately. It'd mean that everything else was fine too.

The call didn't go through. Clara's heart dropped. She returned the phone and thanked Jessica.

She tried to raise the subject again at dinner. David brushed her off.

"Probably a tree fell on the lines. They'll fix it soon enough."

David, of course, knew better. *It must be exhausting*, Clara thought, *to be the world's leading expert on everything.*

By Thursday nothing had changed. Clara called every day, reaching out to everyone she knew back home. She even once called Sophie's old school just to see if it would connect. It didn't.

In Fairbanks everything seemed to work. On Wednesday David mentioned that one of his colleagues had spoken with family in Georgia without issue. Whatever the problem was, it had to be local.

"Trash pickup was missed," David announced, sitting down for dinner as if it were somehow Clara's fault.

She didn't reply. What was there to say? She turned to her son instead.

"How's school?" Clara asked Caleb, who was picking at his food, his bored expression radiating disdain toward the simple meatballs and mashed potatoes. Sophie had stayed home with a fever that showed no sign of letting up.

Caleb shrugged, murmuring something inaudible, rationing his words as if they cost him money.

His phone lay next to his plate. When a new message flashed across the screen, Clara caught a glimpse of his wallpaper: a photo of him with the girl he was seeing. Caleb noticed her looking and quickly flipped it over.

Clara ignored it. "So everything's good?"

Another hum.

She wondered how he spoke to anyone else. Did he actually form words, whole sentences, when it wasn't his family? Or was it only with them that language became such a burden?

"How's Naya?" she asked, keeping her tone casual.

David, absorbed in whatever he was reading on his phone, didn't look up.

That's when Caleb snapped. "What's with all the questions? What are you, the Gestapo?" He pushed his plate back. "I'm done. Can I be excused?"

David finally lifted his eyes. "How are you speaking to your mother?"

"Why's she prying?" Caleb shot back.

"She's just making conversation."

Clara wasn't sure how to feel about David's defense. It only seemed to set Caleb off further. He slouched in his chair, arms folded tight across his chest, glaring at the table.

The lights went out. Darkness swallowed the room. For a long, frozen moment, no one moved.

Then Sophie's voice broke through the dark. "Mommy I'm scared," she whispered.

"It's all right. The generator will start in a second," David said softly. And almost on cue the low hum began, followed by the lights flickering back on.

"What was that about?" Clara asked, though she knew no one could answer.

Caleb, forgetting his earlier irritation, stood and peered out the window.

"The whole neighborhood's out."

One by one generators rumbled to life across the street, squares of light returning to the houses. Clara had hoped the outage would end before bedtime, it didn't. Power cuts weren't unusual, but with the cell service sputtering and the garbage that never got picked up it felt like a bad omen. She kept telling herself she was imagining it.

David snored beside her, and she forced her eyes over the same unread page of a book she hadn't touched in months. The house kept making noises. When the temperatures first plummeted, sleep became impossible. She lay awake, searching on her phone: *Why is my house making that noise? Is it safe?*— refusing to accept that this was normal. This wasn't floorboards creaking. It was sharp cracks, sudden pops, and at times a wet, echoing drip that sounded too loud to belong to plumbing. She was certain the place was coming apart around her.

By morning, when her husband's alarm went off, the generator had stopped. The power was back on.

After David left for work, Clara tried calling her sister, then her mother again. The line stayed quiet. Sophie had come home with a cough that was getting worse by the hour, so Clara strapped her to the nebulizer prescribed by her old doctor in North Carolina. She set the girl in front of the TV, attached to the machine, and decided it would be okay to make a quick run to the store. Back home her mom would usually watch Sophie when she went out, here she had no choice but to leave her alone. A babysitter wasn't something they could afford. She could have asked Caleb, though he hadn't come back from school yet. It wasn't unusual. Sometimes he stayed late for after-school activities, the wilderness club, or just hanging out with friends. He was always home before curfew, so she wasn't worried.

The aisles were eerily bare. Worse than the day before. A couple of women drifted slowly between the shelves, their faces echoing the same quiet frustration Clara felt. The egg section remained empty and it wasn't just that. Most others were sparse, especially the fresh produce. Clara usually stuck to self-checkout to avoid too much human contact; today she abandoned the habit and went straight to the cashier. While a weary woman with thin mouse-gray hair scanned her items, Clara asked, forcing her voice to stay casual so she didn't sound like one of those hysterical women making a scene, "What's going on with all the empty shelves?"

"Deliveries. The snowstorm probably slowed the truckers," the woman replied with a shrug so indifferent that Clara thought even if a meteorite were hurtling toward Earth to destroy all life, the cashier would still be scanning items with the same expressionless, tired face.

Back in the car, Clara sent another message to her mother and sister. Again the red circle appeared beneath it, as it had all week. Only now did she notice her own screen—no bars in the upper right corner, no Wi-Fi, just an SOS signal. Dead zone.

She toggled airplane mode, waited, then switched it off. No

changes. She restarted the phone and waited again. Still the same. Frustrated, she shoved the useless piece of plastic into her purse and glanced around, unsure what to do.

The parking lot was nearly empty, though it was never crowded at this hour. A woman pushed a cart loaded with frozen pizzas and energy drinks. The world remained its usual dull gray.

That strangely steadied her. She started the car and pulled out of the parking lot, merging into the quiet streets covered in snow, the lines barely visible.

Once she got home she tried her laptop. No Wi-Fi. Maybe, she thought, the same provider handled both phone and internet. Without a signal the world felt wrong, as if its rules had quietly shifted. Clara caught herself wondering when constant connection had become the baseline of living. As a child no one had expected to reach her at school or know where she was every second, and it had been fine.

*It's going to be fine.*

*When David gets home he'll sort it out.*

For now she just needed to be patient and keep herself busy.

**2**

# CLARA

She hoped to catch her neighbor outside and ask, but the driveway stayed empty.

*Right. They're probably at work.*

Hours dragged on. Clara made Sophie a quick snack, then went back to the window. The storm had worsened, snow falling in thick, blinding sheets.

Caleb still hadn't returned.

"Let me see your phone," she told Sophie.

Clara had made sure Sophie got a phone when she started kindergarten. Between her health and all the news about school shootings, she didn't want to take any chances. David, however, was strongly against it. He said she was far too young for a phone. It was true. None of the other kids had one yet, not even now among eight-year-olds, and especially not back then when they were much younger. But Sophie needed it. What if the teacher didn't notice Sophie had trouble breathing? At least then she could call her mother to come to her rescue. They argued for days. In the end it was Clara's mother who lost patience and bought Sophie the phone. David had been so furious he nearly threw it out.

No signal. The girl didn't even notice. Her phone settings only allowed her to contact her parents and receive calls or texts from them.

Clara felt a tight knot form in her chest and turned away so Sophie wouldn't notice. She busied herself with the dishwasher, forcing her hands to move. The effort didn't last. Halfway through she found herself drifting back to the window, searching for any sign of Caleb. She moved to dusting, only to stop at the scattered toys Sophie had left behind. Clara drifted from one task to another, never finishing anything. She kept jumping at the sound of passing cars, hoping it was Caleb, and each time it wasn't she found herself silently scolding him for making her worry.

David came back from work and Clara was on him the second the door opened.

"Do you have phone service? None of ours is working. Did we forget to pay for the phones and the internet? It won't even connect to Wi-Fi."

He raised his eyebrows, hung his coat with deliberate calm, and pulled his phone from his pocket. Clara nearly vibrated with impatience as he flicked through the screen, toggling airplane mode like she had done a dozen times already.

"I tried restarting mine. Sophie's too. Nothing."

"Let me see."

David sat at the counter, shoes still on, one lace untied, with all three phones laid out in a neat row. He swiped, checked, and frowned. Clara felt her shoulders relax, relieved to have relinquished control to another adult, someone who could take charge. David didn't always make the choices she wanted—like moving states—but he was better at navigating obstacles.

"Hm," he said after a pause. "Have you checked the modem?"

Clara hadn't. The strange box with lights scared her and she dusted carefully around it, afraid that if she touched it, she'd break something.

David went to the box by the TV, fiddled, cursed under his breath.

"Nothing either. Must be the tower."

"Do you think it'll be back tomorrow?"

"Maybe. I wish we had a landline."

"Yeah," she said staring out into the night. The neighbors' windows were dark. No porch light either. Odd. They always left it on. Maybe they'd gone out, she told herself.

"Where's Caleb?" David's voice cut in.

Clara shuddered, a pang of guilt coursing through her for momentarily forgetting that Caleb hadn't come home. She felt distracted and unfocused, a gnawing sense that something was terribly wrong. Like the quiet before a storm in a horror movie— nothing had happened, but she knew the danger was already there, waiting to strike.

"I don't know. He didn't come home from school. I tried calling …"

"What do you mean you don't know?" David interrupted her.

"I figured he was with Naya and since the phones are out …" She snapped, "I was going to tell you."

David was already pacing, grabbing his coat again. "Where does she live?"

"In a village up north. I think he said it was about fifteen miles outside Fairbanks. The name is in my phone ... somewhere." She scrolled through her notes, hands trembling, but it wasn't showing, lost among grocery lists and notes. "I think it's called Nanana, or was it Tanana? Something with *ana*."

David was running out of patience and Clara felt it, her hands trembling even more. She knew he would blame her. He always did anytime one of the kids did something wrong, as if it were her fault, as if she hadn't watched them closely enough, hadn't been a good enough mother. Cut off from the world she had no way of knowing if Caleb was okay. David snatched the phone from her and strode out. The door slammed behind him, the sound striking her like a sharp slap. The car rumbled to life, and red taillights blinked in the window before disappearing into the snowy night. The house sank into silence.

Sophie hovered by the stairs, hugging the railing.

"Is something wrong with Caleb?"

"No sweetheart. Daddy's just going to pick him up. He probably lost track of time."

"The TV's not working," Sophie said.

Right. Clara remembered the DVDs and reluctantly felt grateful to David for being so meticulous about buying them instead of relying on subscription services. They still had one or two so Clara wasn't too bored at home, and the kids could watch something they wanted. With the lines down that wasn't an option.

"We'll put a DVD on," she said, smiling at her daughter and pointing to the collection.

It took her several minutes to find a cartoon Sophie had watched before and didn't mind seeing again. All the while Clara kept glancing at the clock, her mind tightening with each passing minute, silently wishing David and Caleb would come home.

She tried to reason with herself. Caleb was sensible, not reckless. But he was still a boy, still capable of mistakes. She thought of herself at that age, the lies she told, the places she went where she wasn't supposed to be. That was when she had lost her virginity, and God knew it was only by a miracle she didn't get pregnant. Safety had felt distant then, something she believed would never happen to her.

They never had *The Talk* with Caleb. Maybe they should have sat him down and explained sex, the bees, and the flowers. Before, it had felt too early, then it felt too awkward. Now Caleb was dating that girl. From anyone he had chosen her. Clara was not a racist, of course not. She just understood how different those people, Naya's people, were. How vast the cultural gulf between them. She didn't like to think of it, but part of her worried Caleb might change, might take on ways she couldn't understand, habits she'd never accept. Ideally, she thought, he would settle down with someone from his own background, someone she could trust her son with, a girl raised like them with a family she could respect. Naya was an outsider and outsiders were ... unpredictable, for lack of a better word. Besides Clara was only thirty-eight, too young to be a grandmother. Right now Clara would take the chaos of a teenage pregnancy over the unthinkable.

When she was twelve a little boy went missing in their neighborhood. His parents didn't act until it was clear he was gone. They called other parents to see if he was with them, then searched on their own, and only after that contacted the police. The search didn't begin until near dawn. His body was found the next morning at the bottom of a well by an abandoned house where children were strictly forbidden to play. The officers said he'd survived the fall for a short while before dying from his injuries. If only they'd found him sooner.

*Not my child. Not my child. Not my child.*

Clara stared at the window, at the blackened neighbor's house, and felt the same dread bloom in her chest.

*Not Caleb. God, please. Not my child.*

She needed to push the thoughts away and concentrate on other things, mundane things. Sophie had to go to bed. It was getting late. Maybe they could find a book to read together. Reading would calm Sophie and it might steady Clara, too, far better than the noise of cartoons flickering across the screen.

The girl fell asleep quickly. Clara sat by her daughter's bed, listening to her uneven breathing, unwilling to leave. It felt like all the world's peace had gathered here with Sophie. Clara was afraid that if she stepped out, it would scatter.

She lingered in the dark, the book still open on her knees. At every sound of a car outside, her eyes darted toward the window, but it was always someone else. Every so often, she checked her phone again, as if repetition might coax the signal back. She imagined the relief of it, calling David, making sure Caleb was okay and letting the fear drain away. This didn't happen.

The slam of a car door jolted her awake. The book slid from her lap as she lurched out of the chair, nearly tripping in her rush down the hall. For a split second she thought she'd heard Caleb's voice—imagined or real she couldn't tell—David's sharp tone cutting him off, their son muttering back. She almost welcomed the idea of alcohol on his breath, cigarettes, weed—*no doubt that girl's given her people were known for smoking*—something stupid, survivable. A teenage mistake they could argue about in the morning.

When she reached the door David stood alone, brushing snow from his hair. She felt as if the air had been punched out of her.

"Did Caleb come home?" David asked, stamping snow from his boots.

Clara's first thought was stupid, automatic, that if he'd tracked in that much snow just walking from the driveway the morning would be worse. Then his words sank in.

She broke. Tears came hard, her chest collapsing with them. It was night. Caleb hadn't made it home. David hadn't found him. Something was terribly, irreversibly wrong.

David didn't take off his coat, didn't try to console her. He just let out a heavy sigh and opened the door again.

"He wasn't at Naya's?" Clara asked as he stepped out.

"I never made it there. GPS is out. No one around to ask in this goddamn place. The ice fog came down thick. I could barely see the road. I was driving in circles, almost lost myself."

"Okay ..." Clara whispered glancing out the window. Under

the streetlamp, the fog hung thick. Something she'd never seen before. *Fog, in the dead of winter?*

"What should we do?" she asked.

"*I*'m going to the police," he said, putting weight on going without her.

Anger surged through her. She was sick of being trapped, useless, shut out yet blamed for not doing enough. She wanted to argue, to insist on going with him, but Sophie was asleep in the next room and someone had to stay and check on her. So she swallowed it once again.

What was she supposed to do, just sit and wait? Going to bed felt wrong. How could she sleep when her son was God knows where, cold and alone, maybe even hurt? Maybe even ... *no, I shouldn't even think that.* She lay down on the couch, weeping quietly until exhaustion pulled her under.

David returned in less than an hour. He dropped onto the couch beside her, drained. Clara startled awake, more exhausted than before, sensing his presence before her eyes even opened.

"What did the police say?"

"The station was closed."

Clara sat up. "What do you mean *closed*? Aren't they supposed to be on duty twenty-four seven?"

David shook his head, his shoulders slumped with fatigue. "I don't know what to tell you."

Clara's eyes filled with tears. "Where's my boy?"

She wanted David to pull her close, to open his arms the way he used to. But he didn't.

"I'm going back out," he said, standing. "If I'm not back by morning go to the neighbors and ask to use their phone to call the police."

Then he left again and Clara was alone. She wasn't sure how she would call the police if they were closed, yet she didn't ask. She'd have to figure it out.

She lay on her side, staring at her phone. Maybe a message

from Caleb would slip through, telling her he was fine and just with a friend. The screen stayed blank.

She wished she had been more involved in his school life, taken the time to learn who his friends were, to meet their parents, to know where they lived. Caleb had seemed so grown, managing his own schedule and extracurriculars, rarely needing more than a signature or a ride. He was so self-sufficient that Clara let him be and turned her attention to Sophie, who still depended on her.

Two hours later David returned, even more worn down.

"I've driven everywhere. Not a soul. I'll wait until morning to head to the village. I don't want to risk the roads in the dark. If he's there he's probably safe."

*Probably.*

Clara didn't say a word. She only looked at him with her red, exhausted eyes. He spoke to the floor, not to her.

"I can drive around," she offered.

He shook his head. "It's useless. Besides the streets are all snowed. You'll get into an accident."

David's presence, though somewhat reassuring, still jarred on her nerves. He treated her as if she were helpless, incapable of doing anything on her own. The anger that flared at that was quickly swallowed by fear for Caleb. She thought of the boy who had vanished from her childhood neighborhood, how his parents must have felt in those first hours—terrified, still clinging to hope too. She forced the memory aside, another thought rose in its place.

"What if it's all connected? The phones, the internet, Caleb—"

David finally looked at her, not with kindness. His gaze was sharp, weighed down with annoyance. "What are you talking about?" he said turning away. Without removing his coat he went upstairs, dismissing her as he always did.

For a fleeting second, she wished he would never return.

. . .

Clara barely slept. At first light she slipped into her coat, careful not to wake David, and crossed the street to her neighbors'. Their driveway remained empty.

*Have they gone somewhere?*

Still, she climbed the slippery porch and rang the bell. The chime echoed inside as if the house were completely hollow. Then a cat started meowing loudly. Clara rang again. No footsteps followed. After a few minutes, she knocked hard, her frozen knuckles aching. The mewing continued, but no one was rushing to open the door.

Clara stepped off the porch, pressed her face to the window and peered in. The furniture was in place. The house looked unsettled with clothes strewn across the floor, papers scattered on the table and counters, drawers left half-open as though they'd been packing in a rush. Or maybe they'd been robbed. Or worse.

A chill ran down Clara's spine.

*Maybe I should call the police ...*

She remembered the phones were down. What could she do?

"Amanda? Max? Are you there?" She rapped on the glass, her voice shaking. "My son's missing! Please! I need to use your phone!"

No answer.

Defeated, she stepped off the porch. Clearly no one was home. She turned toward her own house and froze.

A figure stood by the door, shoulders hunched as he fumbled with the lock. Her chest tightened. For a terrible second she thought it was a policeman, come with news too awful to say out loud.

Then he turned, hair falling into his eyes in that familiar, stubborn fringe she'd begged him to cut.

"Caleb!" Clara's voice shook.

She had expected guilt on his face, instead he met her with the same flat mix of indifference and boredom.

"Where have you been?" she nearly screamed. Seeing her son safe, Clara shook all over, her body betraying the flood of emotions she'd tried to hold back. Dread and desperation twisted into raw, furious relief, the kind that makes a parent's first instinct to shout at the child they'd feared lost.

"Can we go inside? You're yelling in the middle of the street." Caleb's calmness only infuriated her more. She almost raised her hand. Clara had never believed in hitting her children. Caleb had only been spanked once in his life when he was eight and ran off with a friend to build tree houses in the woods, coming home hours after dark. Before it could escalate any further, the front door opened and David appeared, exhaustion carved into his forehead, the skin beneath his eyes sagging and discolored. When he saw Caleb shadows deepened across his face, making him look almost like a supervillain from a comic book.

"Get in. Now." His voice left no room for argument.

They gathered in the kitchen. Caleb shook his leg under the table, a habit that could mean boredom or nerves. He'd been doing it since he was a child, and no amount of threats or reminders had ever made him stop. Every time he had to sit down for family time, his leg began to shake uncontrollably, to the irritation of his parents.

"Where have you been? Your mother and I were worried sick," David demanded.

Caleb threw up his arms, defensive. "I tried calling but the lines are down! I got stuck at Mike's place when the storm hit and his car wouldn't start. What was I supposed to do?"

Clara closed her eyes. It wasn't really Caleb's fault, just a chain of bad luck: the storm, the dead phones. She wanted to be mad at him, yell, ground him—anything to let the frustration, the fear out, cleanse herself of these emotions.

"You're grounded," David said, turning away. He was already pulling himself back toward work mode.

"The hell I am!" Caleb snapped. "It wasn't my fault! You want me to walk across the city in a blizzard?"

David didn't answer. He wouldn't even look at him.

Caleb turned to his mother, a last resort. "Mom tell him."

Clara only shook her head and laid a hand on his shoulder. She had no strength left for arguments. Besides, David rarely listened to her anymore. He hadn't been listening for a long time, sometimes Clara wondered if this was the end of their marriage. She tried to make herself feel guilty about it, for some reason she couldn't.

"This is bullshit," Caleb muttered, twisting out of her touch and running upstairs to his room.

"Language," she said automatically, though in truth she didn't care. He could rage and sulk all he wanted. What mattered was that he was here, alive, sitting at their kitchen table. The rest was irrelevant.

3

# DAVID

David was tired. Whatever he'd imagined his life would be at forty, this wasn't it. He'd always assumed there'd be a family, a job, some kind of stability, none of it looked the way he once pictured.

Ever since he was a child, he'd been obsessed with the ocean, though he'd never seen it. He grew up in Idaho, son of a miner who worked hard for little pay, with a mother he only ever remembered being sick and bedridden, unable to do anything. They never traveled beyond their town, let alone left the state.

When David was seven, an adult spotted him buried in a book about sharks and slipped a new phrase into his world: marine biologist. Said as a joke, making fun of a kid so deeply absorbed in the underwater world that the book offered, the words stuck. *Marine biologist.* From that moment it became his dream, even if the ocean itself remained a distant mystery.

Although his parents never paid much attention to this obsession, he never quite grew out of it. Life decided for him. He studied hard and applied himself, devouring every biology lesson, memorizing facts about marine life, and spending hours in the library poring over textbooks and articles. Somehow it wasn't enough; he didn't make the cut for college admissions. This nearly broke him. He couldn't imagine himself as anything else, but giving up on college altogether seemed pointless. For a time he considered enlisting in the army or joining the Marines, hoping to earn another chance at an education through military service. In the end he chickened out. A military career seemed too high a price to pay, even for a lifelong dream. He settled for environmental science instead, expecting to find some spark of interest there. He never did. His career became something he coasted through on autopilot because he didn't know what else to do, and it was too late to change course.

He met Clara when they were barely twenty. She wasn't in college—had dropped out of high school and was working at a coffee shop. She used to say studying wasn't for her, that she'd rather make her own way in the world than waste years and money just to start from scratch. Unlike him she carried herself lightly, seemingly immune to the weight of expectation. Unlike him she had her family. She refused to move too far from them, which proved useful once Caleb was born, then Sophie. Her mother was always there, helping with the kids and the housework. Said help came at a high cost to everyone's peace of mind. When she cared for the children she refused to follow the rules Clara and David had agreed on. She insisted on doing things her own way, constantly pointing out what she thought they were doing wrong. If David tried to argue she'd grow upset, saying, "I'm just trying to help! If it were up to you, you wouldn't let us speak at all!" Her words left David feeling like a powerless despot in his own home.

She scolded Clara constantly, making her feel miserable and, at the same time, draining her of the will to do anything at all. Clara had always wanted to be a psychologist, but convinced herself she was too stupid for school after failing a couple of classes. David disagreed, saying that if she'd applied herself more the results would've been different, only by then it was too late. They had children, his student loans, credit cards, and sending Clara back to school would mean taking on more debt. Even so David would have done it. He would have done anything to help Clara break free from her toxic family, get an education, and build her own life—without them. Of course, Clara's mother and sister insisted that her life now had far greater purpose because of her children, that education was only a distraction.

Despite all that they were there for her. David had no such safety net. His father was, as far as he knew, still alive, drinking himself into oblivion somewhere in Idaho. They hadn't spoken since David left for college. Not out of any fight, they just stopped calling. Sometimes he thought about picking up the phone, but the longer he waited the harder it became. His mother had died of cancer when he was thirteen, and after that his father was rarely sober. David remembered hiding bottles, once even pouring the whiskey down the sink. He remembered the beating that followed too.

Yet he didn't like Clara's family, and the feeling was mutual. What had first seemed like warmth and closeness was, in truth, a toxic codependence. Clara told her mother everything, and David suspected she shaped those stories in ways that always cast him as the bad guy. It irritated him and he took it out on Clara, which only made things worse.

Clara with him and Clara with her mother were two different people. A schoolteacher in the past, Clara's retired mother's favorite pastime was teaching others how to live, especially when no one had asked her. David couldn't stand it and always pushed back. Every family meal turned into an argument. Clara was caught in the middle, trapped between two fires. Though she would initially side with David, the argument would drag on for days, making them fight among themselves. Then Clara, like a beaten dog with nowhere else to turn, would go back to her mother and sister, tell them everything in painstaking detail, and try to smooth things over between David and them. All it did was reestablish the quiet mutual dislike that would smolder until the next explosion.

Eventually he stopped trying to discuss it with Clara at all. Their conversations dwindled to logistics—who takes the kids and when—and he threw himself into work.

The years dragged on. Two kids, one marriage that felt less like a partnership and more like a merger. They'd fused into each other, forming a single, solid thing—misshapen, durable, and without purpose.

That might have gone on forever, until the pandemic hit. His firm lost clients. The layoff notice came. Suddenly he was home: two kids, a mortgage, and an unemployed wife who nagged him about something every other hour of the day.

She kept insisting on selling the house before they defaulted on the mortgage and moving in with her mother, whose health deteriorated. After a bad fall and a hip replacement surgery, she could no longer provide childcare; instead requested Clara to come every other day to take care of her.

That was when David discovered the money they'd used for the down payment wasn't Clara's personal savings, but a loan from her mother. The old woman was demanding it back, trying to persuade her daughter to divorce David and become her live-in caregiver. She wanted to turn Clara into her slave.

When the truth came out David was so furious he didn't even yell. Clara had lied to him about the source of the money and now a large portion of their principal, as it turned out, didn't even belong to them. It felt like the only way out of the mess was, indeed, divorce—and for Clara to return to her mother's control.

At that point, strangely, it got better.

They sold the house and repaid Clara's mother, which left them almost penniless. Apparently, Clara had a huge fight with her over them not moving in to be her free sitters, and she stopped visiting altogether. David expanded his job search until he finally landed an offer at the military base in Fairbanks. There was no relocation package, but David was willing to drain what remained of their savings if it meant starting over. Clara opposed the move, clinging to anything familiar she had in North Carolina, though with no real argument and no real say in it. It was a job, a solid salary, enough to keep them afloat and perhaps even buy another house in a few years. He promised her it would only be temporary, that they'd move back once he found a position closer to her family. "Just to save some money," he said. Deep down he knew they weren't coming back. At best, he'd agree to a visit once a year. Or even less.

So they moved. The kids adjusted well to the new place and its climate. Sophie was sick on and off, but he was sure it would pass. David's work on the base paid well enough to pay down the credit card debt they'd accumulated during his months of unemployment and even save a little. Clara was the only one who withered in Fairbanks, and David was convinced it was the result of her own doing. What annoyed him most was that Clara wasn't even trying. For the first time in her life she was far from her toxic mother and sister, and it seemed to hollow her out.

All the while Sophie's health was a constant worry in the back of her mind. Their daughter had already had bronchitis twice since the move, every change in weather seeming to knock her down. David had told himself her body would adjust in time; Clara was making it a bigger problem than it was.

David drove in silence. The perpetual gloom was getting to him too. He missed the long evenings, the sunlight that lingered after work, the warmth of milder weather. But complaining wouldn't change anything, so he kept his thoughts to himself unlike Clara.

The headlights cut through the darkness, illuminating the snow-covered road ahead. Normally he listened to the morning news on his way to work, but the radio had been dead for days. Besides his focus was entirely on the road, which was in much worse condition today. The snowplows clearly hadn't made it this far yet. A dirty layer of snow, smeared and compacted by passing cars, hid the potholes beneath, more treacherous than ever.

After searching for Caleb most of the night, he needed quiet to avoid the headache he felt brewing. All he wanted was to get to the base, settle at his desk, and have a cup of coffee with two ibuprofens. And then, in a couple of hours, two more.

At the base gate David pulled up and waited, staring through the windshield, his mind numb. The guards would rotate, but he was starting to remember them. One asked when the weather started changing, "How's the cold treating you, Olson?" every time they saw each other. Another guard was always silent, checking David's documents with dedicated precision, his face moody and unreadable, making David feel like he didn't quite belong.

It took a minute for David to realize that no one was coming out to him. The booth was dark. No movement. He tapped the steering wheel and gave a short honk. Still nothing. Leaning forward he squinted through the windshield, the booth looked deserted.

He rolled down the window, and the wind knifed into the car flinging icy snow across his face. He honked again, louder this time, then shouted, "Anyone here?" while wincing against the cold.

No answer.

Uneasy, he stepped out and tried the booth door. Locked. He cupped his hands against the glass and squinted inside. Empty chair. Mug on the counter. Half a newspaper folded neatly. It looked like someone had just stepped away, yet no one came back.

*What the heck? This can't be right.*

He sat in the car, heater blasting, still shivering—not from the cold, but from a creeping empty feeling, like being alone in a cemetery at night. The world around him felt unreal, suspended.

Had something happened last night while their phones were still dead? Was there another pandemic he hadn't heard about? Another lockdown? If the storm had been worse than they thought, maybe the base had been evacuated. Why hadn't anyone come to town though?

He turned off the car and stepped out again. Then he did the unthinkable: Walked into the military base without showing a single piece of documentation.

The parking lot stretched ahead with just a handful of cars, each one buried under a crust of snow. They must have been sitting there all night. Not a single person in sight. No security patrol. No footsteps. No voices. Nothing.

At the main building he swiped his badge. The reader blinked red. He tried again, slower. Red. He pressed the card harder against the scanner. Remained red.

"Motherfucker," David muttered.

He turned in a slow circle, scanning the grounds. At this hour the place should have been alive—soldiers in formation, workers hurrying to their posts, trucks growling through the gates. Instead it was dead, only the flag snapping and flapping violently in the wind above the barren yard.

In college he'd known a guy with a fear of empty places, who would panic and sweat profusely even in a deserted corridor. In this instant David understood the feeling. A familiar place, stripped of people, took on a menacing presence, as if the emptiness itself were alive. Uncanny.

He tried another entrance. Another locked door. Another flash of red.

The icy gust cut through his coat and his fingers ached even inside thick gloves. He must have been wandering the grounds longer than he'd realized. There was nothing else he could do.

He dashed back to his car, fumbling with the key, eyes fixed on the gates, and then sped away feeling as though something was chasing him.

**4**

# DAVID

Clara wasn't home, her car gone. The breakfast dishes sat on the counter and the coffee pot was still warm, but the house was silent. No Clara. No kids.

Just like the military base.

David had never been prone to panic; now, with all the strange events piling up, it was hard to keep it at bay.

"Clara?" he called into the empty house, already knowing there'd be no answer.

He pulled out his phone to call her, then remembered tech devices were dead. His rage flared. He was about ready to smash the useless piece of plastic against the wall. Where was everyone? Had aliens shown up and taken people while he slept?

Finally he caught himself. It was morning. Clara must have driven Caleb and Sophie to school, or maybe gone to the store. This of course didn't explain the abandoned military base. Phones had gone out four days ago. Then Wi-Fi. Then GPS. Now the base was deserted.

Was it all connected?

David thought of himself as a practical man. The world wasn't complicated—messy yes, not hard to understand. Usually the simplest explanation was right. Here there wasn't one. In any other situation he'd be a go-getter, a doer, someone who grits his teeth and pushes through. Today, without his job and alone, he didn't know what to do or how to apply himself. For the first time in a long while, he felt utterly lost.

An hour later Clara came through the door, frantic, to find David still sitting at the counter, unmoving.

"The school bus never showed. I had to drive the kids. And then at the store cards didn't work! None of the payment systems are working. Thank God I had cash. And the shelves—half bare. Wait … what are you doing home?"

"Something's happened," David said. "The base was empty. Completely."

Clara set the grocery bags down slowly. "What do you mean *empty*?"

"Deserted. Not a soul."

She frowned. "Max and Amanda are military, aren't they? The neighbors? They should know something. Only … they weren't home this morning either. What do you think is going on?"

David rubbed his face, exhaustion weighing down his body. "I don't know."

"Do you think it's another virus? Should we get the kids?"

"I don't know Clara."

He glanced at the bags. "You said the store was half empty?"

"Yeah."

"You mean empty of people or empty of food?"

"No food. Plenty of people. Everyone's shopping like it's Black Friday."

David stood. "We should go back. Now."

Clara stared at him. "What's going on? Can we at least unpack the groceries first?"

"No." His voice was flat. "Let's go."

Clara kept nibbling at him throughout the drive, complaining about everything: the school bus system, services being down for days, the roads that were practically impassable. "I could barely drive! With the kids in the car! Dangerous! I'll be writing a complaint as soon as we get the internet back! This is unacceptable!" She didn't even notice that David hadn't said a word, hadn't even glanced at her, just kept his eyes on the road forcing himself not to snap, not to tell her to shut up and let him think.

The supermarket hit them with a strange stillness. The fluorescent lights hummed overhead, throwing a harsh glow on half-vacant shelves. Shoppers moved down the aisles, rushed, carts filled with odd assortments—whatever was left.

"It's worse now," Clara said under her breath.

A woman rolled past with a cart piled high with canned beans and bags of flour.

"Get canned food," David said grabbing an abandoned cart. His voice was clipped, urgent. "Anything non-perishable. Rice, lentils, dried beans. Spam. High calorie. As much as you can carry."

Clara hesitated and he could see the questions rising, but his stern expression must have warned her off. She had likely never seen him like that. He was the steady one. The rock. His wife slipped into the aisles without protest.

David scanned the store for answers. He spotted a woman with a name tag that read "Sarah, Store Manager" pushing a cart stacked so high with food that a few cans tumbled to the floor. He approached as she bent to pick them up, shoving them back in place and steadying the pile with one hand.

"Excuse me," he said forcing his voice to stay even. "What's happening? The shelves are almost empty."

Sarah clutched the pack of pasta she'd just picked up from

the floor like a lifeline. "We haven't been getting shipments this week. No trucks."

"That's unusual."

Her eyes flicked around the store. "Could be the weather. We're supposed to get a delivery tonight." She managed a thin smile. "Sorry for the inconvenience."

David thanked her and walked off, already calculating how much cash he had on him. Without waiting for him to disappear around the corner, Sarah rushed her overflowing cart through the Employees Only door, the food vanishing with her.

When he found Clara, her cart was nearly empty. His was half full.

"Are you insane?" Clara whispered. "What are we going to do with all this?"

He dumped more bags into her cart without answering.

"David!" she pressed, her voice rising. "Can you talk to me? What's going on?"

"Later. Just grab what you can. Go."

At checkout, the process dragged. With the card readers down, the cashier had to ring each item by hand. David nearly emptied his wallet.

They left in silence, pushing their rattling carts across the lot, the sound harsh in the frozen air. Only when the groceries were loaded into the car did Clara finally ask, voice low, "Do you think it's serious?"

David started the engine. "I don't know. But I'd rather be ready."

They drove without speaking.

A Fred Meyer's truck sat half in their lane. David slowed, then stopped.

"What are you doing?" Clara asked.

"It's the store's truck. Driver's still inside." He got out before she could protest.

The cab door was ajar. A man climbed out, his movements sluggish, shoulders hunched against the cold.

"You alright?" David called.

The trucker's face was drawn, his voice flat. "Ran out of gas. I was headed to Anchorage but ..." He shook his head.

"What happened?"

"Stations were closed. Three of them. No fuel anywhere. Turned back but didn't make it." His eyes flicked briefly to Clara. "You know if there's another station nearby? One that might still have a landline?"

David nodded toward the car. "Come with us. We'll try."

The man introduced himself as Jensen. Clara trailed after them, tense, her gaze never settling. David was ever so slightly annoyed, mostly out of habit, because now she wasn't in the way and stayed silent. Nothing to snap at her about.

David used the time while they were driving to ask as many questions as he could.

"Did something happen with your route? Any road closures?"

Jensen thought for a beat. "No, nothing I can think of. The only thing that stood out was how many cars were leaving town and the empty gas stations. Town after town no gas."

"Just out of gas or closed completely?"

"Some closed. Some open but empty. Like everything ran dry at once. Something's going on I'm telling you. It's the government. Probably a war. Or worse. And us little folks? They don't even bother to tell us."

David felt Clara tense up next to him, said nothing.

He remembered a small station on the outskirts, open the night before when he was searching for Caleb, somewhere on the way to the village. When they pulled up, a faint light still glowed inside. A hand-painted sign in the window read: Open 24/7.

"Lucky break," Jensen muttered. Relief softened his face.

The gas station was small and worn, its wooden walls

creaking under the weight of years. Inside narrow aisles were packed with an odd mix of goods: shelves sagging under canned food, jars of preserves, stacks of firewood, and a few racks of basic clothing. The air smelled faintly of gasoline and coffee. Behind the counter an elderly man emerged, his face lined and weathered. A handwritten note taped to the glass read: Cash only. Sorry.

Jensen paid for the diesel and insisted on covering David's as well, saying it was for his kindness. David hated accepting—he'd only helped Jensen because he was hoping to get some answers. With their cash running low, he didn't argue.

"Landline?" Jensen asked.

"Down for days," the man replied. "No connection at all."

David pressed, "Heard anything about deliveries being stopped?"

"Nothing. Haven't seen a soul. We're out of the way here."

David bought two fuel canisters with their remaining cash. Clara tried to object, but David waved her off as if she were an annoying fly. She stayed in the car, rigid in the passenger seat, jaw clenched and eyes averted, refusing to watch their savings slip away.

Back at the stranded truck, snow already dusted the hood. Jensen took the diesel with a grim nod.

"It'll get me moving and then we'll see."

David forced a jagged clearing of his throat, buying himself a few seconds to decide what to say. "We're lucky this station still has gas."

Jensen gave a weary smile. "Luck is running thin these days."

**5**

# CLARA

As Jensen walked back to his truck, Clara turned to David. "What do we do now?"

David hesitated, then gripped the wheel. "Let's go get the kids. I'm not sure how safe it is outside."

"What do you think is going on?" Clara asked quietly.

"I don't know!" David snapped, slamming his palms against the top of the wheel.

She knew how much he hated it when she demanded answers he didn't have. She also knew he wasn't as mad at her as at his own inability to do anything.

As they pulled into the school parking lot Clara's chest tightened. It was far too early for pickup yet even then the visitor lot, normally holding at least a few cars from volunteering parents, was eerily empty. No kids playing out back during recess. One school bus sat at the curb, its doors yawning open, snow already drifting inside.

It looked eerily similar to a scene from a zombie movie, where a character wakes to the collapse of society. Clara shuddered.

David acted as if he didn't notice or perhaps preferred not to react. His shoulders stayed squared, his gaze fixed ahead, jaw clenched. Clara trotted behind him, the crunch of snow under her boots breaking the silence, but he made no effort to slow his pace. She kept glancing up at him, unsure whether to speak, afraid her words might make him explode.

They slipped in through the front doors without a sound. No one was there to stop them. Clara's heart sank. If they could get in so easily it meant anyone could. And with gun violence on the rise it wasn't a good sign.

*No, no, no, no, no, no, no.*

She kept repeating it in her head, frantically scanning the hallway, searching for bloodstains, scattered school supplies, anything—and finding nothing to her huge relief. The hall was clean and deserted.

"Sophie?" Clara called, losing patience. She needed to say something, to release this tension, and screaming her daughter's name felt like the only reasonable option.

Her voice echoed through the halls, venturing into empty classrooms with chairs overturned and loose papers scuttling across the linoleum in the draft like startled insects.

Clara's pulse quickened with every empty room they passed, dread pressing heavier against her chest. Tears stung her eyes. *Not my little girl. Not Sophie. Please.* It had turned out fine with Caleb, so it'd probably be the same now. Right? There was always a reasonable explanation. Always.

The sound came from further down the hall: the squeak of shoes on linoleum, a hushed scuffle, the low rumble of a voice. From behind the heavy gym doors came distant, muted noises of children, a collective rustling and murmuring like a restless hive of bees. The air inside smelled faintly of kids' sweat, dirty shoes, and the slightly sour tang of lunchboxes left too long in lockers.

Clara rushed in and pushed the doors open. Dozens of children sat on the gym floor, scattered among backpacks and jackets. Some whispered quietly, trading snacks or flipping through worn books; others laughed and talked, indifferent to what had been happening. Clara caught a few children staring ahead, their little faces tense as if they were expecting the worst, as if they knew something terrible was happening.

The way they were all packed into the gymnasium reminded Clara of war zone footage she had seen online: cities under siege, shelters filled with displaced families, parents shielding their children from bombings, classrooms turned into refuges. She had once dismissed those videos, convinced they were staged. But this—this was real.

The substitute teacher, Mrs. Johnson, paced by the bleachers, her face tight with nervous exhaustion, while the janitor leaned against the wall, arms crossed, keeping watch or perhaps just resting, refusing to involve himself in the futile task of controlling a group of restless elementary school children. Clara noticed, almost in passing, how strange it was that a single teacher was responsible for the entire school.

Mrs. Johnson's eyes darted to Clara, relief flooding her features. "Oh, thank God! We've been trying to reach the parents, but ..." She trailed off, gesturing helplessly. "Nothing's working. No phones, no messages."

"Sophie!" Clara called desperately, her eyes scanning the crowd, though none of the faces were familiar.

The children glanced somewhere behind her, and Clara heard a cough. There, slumped against the wall, her daughter's fragile frame trembled in a bout of severe coughing. Even from across the gym, Clara could hear the faint, wheezing rasp of each breath. Her insides churned.

She sprinted to Sophie's side, dropping to her knees. "Sweetheart I'm here," she whispered brushing damp hair back from her clammy forehead.

Sophie's eyes fluttered open, glassy and unfocused. "Mom ... it hurts to breathe," she rasped, each word a struggle. Clara looked back at David, fury in her eyes, *I told you so. I told you she was sick. I told you the phones weren't working. I told you something was wrong. I told you we never should have moved to Alaska.*

She was at her breaking point. David, equally worried, ignored her and spun toward the substitute. "What the hell is going on here?"

The young woman looked on the verge of tears, her voice pitched too high, each word almost shouted, "I don't know! I was supposed to teach second grade. I was monitoring when the kids arrived but no one else came to work except me and Mr. Harris! And I had no way to reach anyone! Can you help get the other parents here?"

"Do you have their addresses?" David asked.

Clara's nostrils flared. They needed to get out of here, get Sophie to safety, and all he could think about was some other woman instead of their own family.

The teacher hesitated. "I'm not sure. They're probably in the files …"

"Can't you just ask the kids?" Clara interrupted, impatient to leave.

David glanced back at Clara, Sophie cradled in her arms. The girl looked pale, her eyes dull and glassy, each exhale carrying a thin, wheezing sound.

"My child is very sick," David said, his voice low, apologetic, and Clara almost groaned.

The woman's hands dropped to her sides. She lost interest in them immediately and walked away, hushing the children and consoling someone who had started crying.

In the car, Clara kept glancing back at Sophie, who seemed on the verge of losing consciousness, her breathing growing more labored with every passing minute, her face pale and drawn. She touched her forehead and felt the heat. Fever.

"Mom, what's that rattling?" Sophie asked weakly, disturbed

by the noise from the trunk. The cans must have fallen out of the bags and scattered all over.

"Just groceries, honey," Clara said softly.


The high school was different. Cars were scattered haphazardly, some with doors hanging open, others still idling. Students loitered outside, jackets unzipped, their breath visible in the cold. No teachers patrolled the lot. No adults tried to impose order.

"Caleb!" David called out. A few kids glanced at him with dull curiosity before turning back to their music, their vapes, their chatter. Engines ran wastefully, chewing through dwindling gas.

Finally, they spotted Caleb near a beat-up 4Runner, something from the '90s. Naya leaned against the driver's side door, her dark hair whipping in the wind, her thick fur-lined parka open, woolen mittens peeking from her sleeves. Clara thought how young she looked, barely seventeen, but her eyes were serious, deep with a knowing Clara found unsettling as if the girl had lived more of life than she ever would.

Naya noticed them first and signaled to Caleb with the point of her sharp chin. Clara hated it. It looked as if the girl were warning him of some unseen danger. Caleb turned, surprised and even a little guilty, quickly masked it with defiance.

"What's going on here?" David demanded.

"Hi, Mr. Olson," Naya said quietly.

David barely nodded.

Naya edged closer to Caleb, folding her arms on her chest.

*She knows we don't like her,* Clara thought. But this was no time for self-reflection and ceremonies.

"How should I know?" Caleb said quickly, and Clara imagined him as a bird that is attacked, rising all his feathers. "There were no teachers. What was I supposed to do? Dad I swear—"

"We came to pick you up. Let's go." David's tone cut him off.

"Dad, I'm going with Naya—"

"Caleb. Now." David's voice was sharp. The chaos of the parking lot made his skin crawl. Whatever was happening, this was no place to linger.

Caleb hesitated, glancing at Naya. She gave a worried nod. "I'll see you later."

"Wait—phones don't work!" Caleb said desperately.

"I'll stop by your house in a couple of days if this keeps up," Naya answered, sliding into the car.

Clara almost told her not to, but swallowed it.

Caleb climbed into the back seat, mumbling something unhappy, then his eyes fell on Sophie. She sat hunched over, coughing, her lips cracked and dry, sweat gleaming on her forehead.

"So ..." Caleb said finally. "Is this like an apocalypse or something?"

"What?" Clara turned in her seat.

"Maybe it's World War Three. Or a bomb." Caleb didn't sound like he was trying to provoke them. He sounded spooked, worried. He continued, "That's why we can't reach anyone. They're all dead. Naya said we should be ready for anything because help won't come. Naya said ..."

David winced as though Caleb had said something unpleasant, and Clara felt a surge of solidarity. What did this girl even know to be quoted like that, as if she held the keys to all the world's knowledge?

"Is Granny dead?" Sophie whimpered.

"Stop talking nonsense," Clara shot Caleb a furious look, then softened her tone for Sophie. "Granny's okay. We'll talk to her very soon."

Caleb clicked his tongue in annoyance, slouched deeper in his seat, and stared out the window.

Sophie's body suddenly convulsed with a violent cough, her frame shuddering with each desperate hack. When it passed, her breathing was even more ragged.

"Where's your inhaler?" Caleb asked, his sharp voice softening when he saw her struggle. "Use it."

"He's right, baby," Clara said gently.

With trembling hands, Sophie pulled her glittery backpack into her lap and dug out the inhaler. She shook it and the familiar rattle tightened the knot in Clara's chest. Sophie pressed down and drew in a long breath of mist, though each inhale came with an audible struggle. She held it just like her mother had shown her and then exhaled slowly. The careful, practiced order of it, learned by such a tiny human, squeezed Clara's heart. Sophie didn't deserve this. Why did she have to suffer?

While her daughter sat there a bit calmer and breathing a little easier, though still wheezing, Clara turned in her seat and gently plucked the inhaler from Sophie's hand. It was light. Almost out. They only had one more at home.


David and Caleb were left to unload the car while Clara tended to Sophie. Caleb grew visibly nervous as he stared at the towering pile of cans in the trunk, finally asking, "Dad? What's going on? Is this for real?" and turning to David because ever since he was twelve he rarely addressed Clara first, avoiding conversations with his parents and only approaching them when he needed something—new gadgets, camping gear, anything for school, or once a knife for his 'survival' training, which was obviously a *no*. He'd always gone to David bypassing his mother entirely, which Clara found irritating but never said anything, especially now that Caleb sounded genuinely worried.

Earlier when he'd rambled in the car about rumors swirling at school, he'd sounded spooked yet casual, as if he didn't quite believe them himself and wanted reassurance. Currently, seeing them tense and stockpiling non-perishable food, he looked genuinely scared.

"Just unload the car, Caleb," David said, before Clara could even consider what to respond.

"We gotta get in touch with Naya," Caleb insisted, following him to the kitchen and piling the next load of cans onto the counter. "Maybe they know more."

"Caleb," David said, stopping and pressing a hand to his eyes, "just finish with the groceries."

David didn't get along with Caleb any better than she did; even so she felt out of place whenever they talked, as if the house had filled with more men to ignore and dismiss her. She went to check on Sophie and was quietly closing the door to her room, careful not to make a sound, when David emerged at the top of the stairs.

"Is she asleep?" he asked.

"She needs to go to the hospital," Clara said in a tight voice, ignoring his question. "We also need to stop by the pharmacy and get more of these inhalers. As many as we can "

"How many does she have left?"

"One. And it won't last her long."

"Why didn't you think about it before?" David snapped in a sharp, low voice to avoid waking Sophie.

Clara felt a hard knot of anger tighten in her chest. It was always like this—his blame, his way of making her responsible for everything while never owning his part. Sophie was his daughter too. Why hadn't he been paying attention? Why hadn't he thought ahead? Why hadn't he listened at the gas station when she begged him to save something for emergencies, like this one? He shut her down then and was now pointing fingers.

"Because we couldn't afford it, asshole!" Clara hissed losing all control, her eyes flaring, her hands clenched in fists.

Ever since they had to pay her mother back, which had always been the plan, he'd been angry with her, his fury simmering just below the surface, and she hadn't wanted to poke the bear. She'd kept her mouth shut.

Her mother's health was failing, medical bills kept piling up. Once a teacher, her mom had been let down by the system—her pension cut drastically. Clara couldn't understand why David refused to accept or even acknowledge it.

Clara had been angry as well. But for the sake of their marriage, for the sake of their children, she swallowed it over and over, hoping it would dissolve.

It didn't.

Silence turned to resentment, and resentment hardened in her chest like a precious stone forming in darkness into something she couldn't name. Something heavy.

She expected David to shout back, to get angry, instead he just stood there silent. Defeated. His shoulders sagged, his hands curling into loose fists at his sides.

"I know we don't have cash left," Clara continued, her frustration growing at his lack of words. *Is that it,* she thought. *Is this the only time you have nothing to say? When you actually need to do something?*

"Let her rest and we'll see how she feels later," David finally said.

Clara exhaled, half-relieved, half-disheartened. She wished he'd said something else that would've let her know he was there for her too. She studied his face trying to conjure the image of the boy she had once loved so completely, without hesitation or doubt, and couldn't. The man standing in front of her was someone else. Yet she was willing to meet him halfway—if only he would take a step toward her.

He didn't. He turned away, muttered "alright then," and went downstairs, where Caleb was waiting by the staircase looking lost. Clara followed reluctantly, arms crossed over her chest, lips pressed tight. The groceries lay scattered across the counter and dining table.

"What's going on?" Caleb asked again, this time without his usual teenage entitlement, without that tone that made it sound like the world owed him answers. He was also scared, his fingers drumming a staccato against the staircase railing he gripped.

Clara and David exchanged glances, slipping into their joint parental faces.

"We don't know," David finally said. "But it doesn't look good. We don't want you to panic or scare your sister. We need you to be an adult right now, alright?"

Caleb nodded and then asked quietly, "Do you think something happened to Gran and Aunt Lisa?"

Clara sighed. "We don't know either. I wish we could tell you more. We just hope they're okay and that whatever this is gets fixed soon."

"This won't last," David added trying to sound convincing. "The authorities will surely do something. They're probably already working on restoring the network and clearing the roads."

"Naya said they won't do anything. That they've already fled. Her uncle said—" Caleb started but David cut him off.

"You need to stop that, Caleb. I can't stand these conspiracy theories. Don't be dumb."

Caleb's nostrils flared, yet he said nothing. He turned, went upstairs, and locked himself in his room.

The day stretched on endlessly. With no connection to the outside world, no news, no messages, no information of any kind. The house felt suspended in time. Clara kept a close watch on Sophie, ready to rush her to the hospital if her condition worsened. David insisted on waiting, worried about wasting gas.

"What if we need it later?" he said. Clara swallowed the urge to ask what *later* meant, or how bad he thought things might get. She knew he didn't have an answer.

Even though she was scared and disoriented by it all, Clara clung to a stubborn hope: Whatever happened had to be fixable. If things were truly catastrophic, they would've heard something by now. People talk. Maybe it wasn't as bad as it seemed. Life would return to normal. They just had to wait.

Caleb sat in his room for a while, listening to music. Clara thought about telling him to turn it down but decided not to light the fuse. He later came out on his own, restless, snapping at them and demanding to be taken to Naya's, insisting she knew better. Clara, exhausted by his whining, was ready to scream. David lost patience first and sent their son back to his room.

Clara stood by the window, her usual vantage point, arms wrapped tightly around her waist.

"They're gone," she murmured just loud enough for David to hear.

"Who's gone?"

"Our neighbors. Amanda and Max. They weren't home last night and this morning I knocked again. Still nothing."

"Maybe they went to see family," David said trying to brush it off.

"Maybe," Clara repeated, her eyes fixed on the empty street.

Maybe not. Earlier loud meowing had drifted over from the house across the street. The cat sounded frantic, clearly in distress. Last time their neighbors had to leave to visit family, they'd asked Caleb to feed their cat for some pocket money. This time they'd left the cat behind and took off without a word. They would either come back soon before the animal starved, or ...

They were military too. And as David had claimed, the base was empty.


Sophie pushed the potatoes around her plate, mashing them with the steamed beans until they merged into an unappetizing mush.

The home-cooked meal seemed to steady everyone, but it wasn't enough to restore normalcy. They ate in silence.

Caleb fidgeted, shifting in his seat, then glanced at his parents from under his brows, head lowered.

"Are we going to help that cat?" he asked at last.

"Caleb just eat your food," his father said.

"But it's going to die!"

"Nobody's going to die Caleb," David replied sharply.

"They'll come back for it," Clara added, trying to soften David's tone and draw Sophie's attention away from the word *death*.

Caleb scowled, brushing his fringe from his face. His leg began to shake uncontrollably. Then, as though forcing the words out before reconsidering, he blurted out, "I want to go live with Naya. In the village."

David set his fork down and rubbed his eyes. Clara glanced at Caleb, startled and caught off guard. He was seventeen. Had he gotten Naya pregnant? Was that what this was about? How were they supposed to deal with it now? Would David say something? That girl was trouble. Clara had known it the moment she'd noticed Caleb wearing a beaded necklace with a pendant, a gift from Naya, as he'd reluctantly admitted when asked. The thought tightened something deep inside her, imagining the girl using her little rituals and trinkets to bewitch her son, making him like her.

David said nothing. He let out a heavy sigh, picked up his fork and continued eating, his calm clearly forced.

"Did you hear me? I'm going to Naya's," Caleb repeated, his voice stronger this time, with no backing out. "I'm staying there. We talked about this."

"Enough," David said. "We're all tired. Enough with your drama."

"I'm not asking, I'm telling," Caleb said, his voice sharper. "Why don't you ever listen? You never listen!"

David slammed his hand on the table. Clara flinched. "You. Are. Not. Going. Anywhere."

"Yes I am!"

"You're seventeen and you'll do what you're told. Stop stressing your mother and sister."

"I'm not a child! And besides why does it even matter? You're all sitting here pretending like everything's fine when everyone else is dead! There's no fucking world anymore!" Caleb shouted.

Sophie stared at him with wide, frightened eyes, on the verge of tears.

"Go to your room," David ordered, his face red with anger.

"Mommy, is this true?" Sophie whimpered. Clara rose from her chair and hurried to her.

"No, baby, he's just joking," Clara said gently.

"Go to your room. Now!" David shouted slamming his hand on the table so hard the plates jumped and his fork clattered to the floor.

Caleb paused, as if expecting his parents to change their minds. Then he stood abruptly, grabbed his plate, and hurled it into the sink. It landed with a deafening crash, shards of ceramic scattering everywhere. Without another word he stormed out, his footsteps pounding up the stairs. His door slammed shut with a violent thud that made Clara wince.

"I swear to God ..." David muttered, his voice tight and controlled, eyes fixed on where Caleb had gone as if sending his rage after him.

"Please don't." She flinched, rubbing her temples as a headache began to build.

## 6

## CLARA

Despite Clara's hopes Sophie was worse in the morning. She looked pale and limp under the blankets, her small body heavy with fever. The room was faintly sour with a child's sweat.

"Mommy …" Sophie's voice was barely a whisper. "I don't feel good. Can I stay home?"

The girl's breathing was labored, each inhale edged with a faint wheeze. Clara's heart lurched when she touched her daughter's forehead, burning hot.

"Oh, baby. Let me look at you," she said softly, trying not to scare Sophie. "Did you use your inhaler last night?"

Sophie gave a weak nod. Clara checked the inhaler. Maybe there was one dose left. They should save it in case Sophie worsened. But Sophie was already struggling and Clara had to act. She set up the nebulizer quickly, coaxing Sophie to breathe in the medication. The wheeze persisted, a harsh rattle in her chest. Clara could almost feel her daughter's oxygen slipping away.

"We need to get you to the hospital," she said, forcing calm into her voice.

She dressed Sophie in fresh clothes, terrified by how her

daughter sagged against her, eyes drooping, too weak to move on her own.

"Can Mr. Whiskers come?" Sophie whispered hoarsely.

"Of course, honey." Clara tucked the stuffed animal into Sophie's arms, then grabbed the medication and medical folder, shoving everything into a bag.

"David?" she called. He emerged from the bathroom with a towel in hand and a wave of irritation washed over her. While she was dealing with their sick daughter, he'd taken his time to wash up. She still hadn't brushed her teeth. Hell, she hadn't even used the bathroom, deciding to check on Sophie before taking care of the basics.

"We're going to the ER," Clara said without preamble.

David knelt beside Sophie, brushed the damp hair from her forehead, and felt for her fever.

"Baby, how are you feeling?" he asked gently.

"Not good. Can't you see?" Clara shot back, her voice snapping like a piece of charcoal. He left the kids to her, trusted her to handle everything, yet he hesitated when she said Sophie needed the hospital.

David stepped back, clearly frustrated by her sudden outburst. She'd always kept her cool with him, patient through his moods and huffing and puffing like a teenager, but now was the worst possible time for his mumbling and hesitation. Their daughter was sick.

"Alright. Pants. Give me one second." For the first time ever, David didn't argue or try to win the argument. He disappeared into the bedroom and Clara heard him dressing in a rush.

She pushed through the front door with Sophie limp in her arms, David close behind. All she saw was the narrow path to the car ahead, until David touched her elbow and stopped her. Clara looked up and saw a beat-up old truck idling at the curb.

"Who's that?" Clara asked, suspicion sharp in her voice.

David's eyes narrowed. "It's Naya."

The driver's door creaked open and Naya stepped out. Her face was tight, unsmiling.

"Hey, Mr. Olson. Is Caleb home?"

David's expression hardened. "Naya, go home. This isn't a good time."

She didn't move. She stepped closer, her voice was calm, serious. "Please, Mr. Olson. I really need to talk to Caleb. It's important—"

"We don't have time for this," David snapped. "Our daughter needs a hospital."

Naya's gaze flicked to Sophie in Clara's arms. Something like fear or pity broke through her face. Then it closed again.

She turned those dark, unblinking eyes toward Clara. "Is she really sick? The hospital won't help. But I know someone who might. Just let me speak to Caleb. I just—"

Clara barked, her voice taut with anger, "Go! Now! Before I call the police!"

Naya's eyes flashed. She cast one last glance at Caleb's window, then turned, climbed into her truck and peeled away, tires spraying snow as she disappeared down the street.

Clara exhaled sharply. David opened the door and she eased Sophie into her seat, buckling her in with a soft, soothing voice. "It's okay, baby. We'll go see the doctor and you'll feel better very soon."

Inside her head, thoughts black and thick as tar churned: *Who does she think she is sneaking around my family? Doesn't she see what's happening?*

The streets were chaotic, coated in snow and ice, unplowed and untreated. They'd seen only a few cars, but the real danger was the road itself. David gripped the wheel with both hands, knuckles white, the car sliding with every turn. Clara kept glancing back at Sophie, swaying in the back seat like a fragile doll, making sure she was all right.

*Almost there*, she kept saying to either Sophie or herself, *almost there.*

When the hospital came into view Clara gasped. Something was wrong. Very, very wrong. Figures in heavy coats moved in slow, tense clusters. No one was coming in or out of the emergency room doors. People seemed distressed, yelling, arguing, pointing at something. Cars sat abandoned at odd angles, doors left open, lights still blinking. A child's bright backpack lay half-buried in the snow, as if someone had dropped it in a rush.

Clara asked David, more from habit than any real expectation of an answer, "What's going on?"

He parked farther away than necessary. "I'll check. Stay in the car," he said without his usual irritation, which only made Clara feel worse. It meant things were really bad.

"We'll go with you. She needs a doctor," she said, her hands shaking as she reached for the car door.

Again, for the second time today, David didn't argue, though Clara had expected him to. He simply waved his hand, a quiet, almost dismissive gesture, and helped Sophie out of the car.

"Can you walk, baby?" Clara asked. Sophie nodded weakly, fever bright in her eyes, her breathing worse than ever.

They pushed through the throng, only to find the sliding doors shut tight.

"What's happening?" David asked no one in particular.

"My mother has cancer," a woman said, voice hollow. "She was supposed to start chemo today. But the hospital's closed."

"Closed?" David echoed.

A man's furious yell split the air: "They're leaving us to die!" The crowd erupted. Accusations flew, voices rising. Then the crash of glass—someone had thrown a stone through the window. An alarm shrieked, no one flinched.

"Take Sophie back to the car!" David shouted over the chaos.

"But she needs a doctor!" Clara cried utterly lost. She heard the man, she knew there were no doctors, her mind refused to accept it.

*There must be ... there has to be ...*

The doors became the mob's focus. A knot of men slammed against them, initially clumsy and disjointed, then falling into a violent rhythm fueled by panic.

"I'll try to grab meds. Go!" he yelled without turning back.

Clara tightened her grip on Sophie and pushed forward through the crowd. Behind them the door rattled under a kick. A sharp scream split the air as though someone had been injured, followed by a desperate cry, "Help! Help!"

Clara didn't see anything. Her vision tunneled; her senses narrowed to the small, gloved hand in hers. They had to get out.

"Help me! Somebody help!" a man kept howling, voice ragged and wet, each scream ripped from a body in pain. Snow whipped across the lot, biting at faces and slicing through coats, feeding on the fear around it. Glass shattered. Metal groaned and screeched.

All Clara wanted was for this to be over, for them to be in the car—or better yet at home in North Carolina, back with her family, safe. And the car was right there, just in front of her.

The keys.

David didn't hand them over.

There was no way they could get inside without breaking the glass. Maybe they could hide behind the vehicle ... Sophie's legs buckled, her small body sagging. Clara spun, her heart seizing. Sophie's eyes were wide, her chest heaving in shallow, gasping breaths.

"Baby, no!" Clara dropped to her knees, pulling her close.

Her fingers fumbled in the bag, frantic for the inhaler. The lining caught, trapping it. Tears blurred her vision as she yanked it free at last. "Breathe, sweetheart, breathe!" Her voice was a broken whisper.

She pressed the inhaler to Sophie's lips, counting, praying, waiting for her chest to rise. Nothing. Just the terrifying stillness of a child's body failing.

Again—shake, press, pray. Again. Shake. Press. Shake. Press. Press. Press. Press. Still nothing. Sophie's lips were turning blue.

"Help! Somebody help!" she screamed, her raw voice slicing through the cold air, dissolving into useless clouds like the man's cries not a minute ago.

Behind them the crowd surged forward, pouring into the building. They didn't hear her, deaf to her pleas and too far away, swallowed by distance and snow. Clara didn't scream for anyone else. She screamed for a miracle. Her voice tore out of her, fueled by a maternal despair so fierce it felt like it could rip her apart, twist her into something unrecognizable. If only she could scream her own life into Sophie …

*Please, God … please don't take my baby …*

A hand gripped her shoulder. Clara whipped her head around to see a woman emerge from the blur, her face worried, serious, untrusting all at once, as if she'd been betrayed before and wanted to make sure Clara wasn't scamming her before offering help.

"What's wrong with her?" the woman demanded.

"She can't breathe! The inhaler …" Clara sobbed, unable to finish. She held up the inhaler in her trembling hand. "Please … please help us."

The woman's eyes flicked to Sophie, then back. "I live right there." She nodded toward a house across the street. "Can you carry her?"

Clara gathered Sophie's limp body against her chest, nodding desperately.

"Then follow me."

The woman led Clara inside, moving through the dim hallway. She pushed open a door where weak streetlight filtered through the curtains. The room was sparse but clean: bare wooden floorboards, a thin rug curling at the edges, a sagging couch with an old quilt folded neatly on top. A single crooked lamp on a side table. A mirror. A door. Another door. The air smelled faintly of disinfectant and boiled tea. Everything seemed carefully tended yet worn down, as if the woman had stopped buying new things long ago. Clara noticed it all in passing, barely registering the surroundings, desperate for help. The woman's slow, heavy movements grated on her nerves. She wanted her to hurry.

"Lay her here," the woman instructed pointing to the couch.

Clara eased Sophie down and stepped back with a heavy heart, letting the woman take charge, trusting a stranger to save her daughter.

The woman checked Sophie's airways and pulse, then placed her hand on the girl's chest to feel her heartbeat. Clara watched her tensely, trying to read her expression—calm and focused, the face of someone who had done this before and learned to stay composed, neither frightening anyone nor offering false hope.

"Can you do something?" Clara's impatience broke through.

"What's her name?" the woman replied steadily.

"Sophie. Is she going to be okay?"

The woman ignored Clara's question and shook the girl gently. "Sophie, can you hear me?"

Clara froze, watching as the woman found a pulse, her voice steady but urgent. "Come on, sweetheart. Wake up. Mommy's here."

They waited in taut silence. Nothing happened. Then Sophie's eyelids fluttered. Her gaze cleared and Clara's knees nearly gave out with relief.

"She's okay," the woman said quietly. "Just not enough oxygen and very cold. But she's breathing."

She then slipped into the bathroom. Clara clutched Sophie's hand, tears spilling unchecked. Cabinet doors banged, packages rustled. The woman returned, cradling a nebulizer.

"Let's get her set up." Her movements were quick, sure, as she fitted the mask. Clara hovered breathless as the first puffs of albuterol hissed into Sophie's lungs.

At last, Sophie's chest rose more evenly. The rasp softened into steadier breaths.

"Better?" the woman asked.

Sophie gave a faint nod.

"Do you like pizza?"

Another nod.

"Pineapple?"

A weak shake of the head. The woman smiled. "Me neither."

Clara laughed once, brokenly, before choking on a sob.

"She's responding well," the woman murmured.

"Are you a nurse?" Clara asked, not knowing what else to say.

"I used to be," the woman replied abruptly, her face hardening.

Clara swallowed and asked the question that had been gnawing at her, "Where did you get this medication?"

"I keep a stash. My daughter has asthma. I couldn't let another child suffer."

Hope surged in Clara. "Could I … buy some from you? Please?"

The woman shook her head gently. "I can't. My daughter needs it. And with all this," she gestured vaguely, a small, noncommittal movement that seemed to mean everything at once, then repeated, "I just can't. Sorry."

The words tore open the black hole in her chest, sucking away the fragile hope before it could even take shape. This was only a reprieve. Sophie would need more, and there might not be any.

"We tried the hospital, but …" Clara faltered.

"They're gone," the woman said quietly.

Clara blinked. "Gone where?"

"I don't know. The staff, the military. They probably evacuated anyone who could be useful."

Clara's lungs stopped. This couldn't be real.

"And you?" she asked, clinging to the hope that if this woman was here, maybe more medical personnel were too. Maybe not all was lost.

"I lost my license," she said looking Clara straight in the eyes, as though she were owning whatever had happened that made her lose it.

Clara's relief at seeing her daughter conscious and breathing began to fade, anxiety creeping back in. Her fingers began to tremble.

"Do you know what's happening?" she blurted. "When will it end? Is help coming? Please tell me help is coming."

The woman didn't answer. She busied herself with putting away the supplies and the precious medication, then spoke over her shoulder in a detached tone, "Fresh ginger tea with honey. Turmeric. Lemon. Eucalyptus steam for her breathing." She glanced at Clara. "Got it?"

Clara nodded numbly.

The woman stood, a quiet signal that her hospitality had run its course and it was time to leave. The moment of shelter slipped away. On top of that, Clara's bladder felt ready to burst.

"Thank you for helping us," Clara said, trying to mask her disappointment. She should be grateful. The woman didn't owe them anything. "Can I use your bathroom real quick before we go?"

The woman waved toward the hallway. "Right side."

Clara hurried down the corridor, her stomach churning with nausea that had nothing to do with food. She shoved the bathroom door closed behind her and finally relieved herself. Her mind felt numb. The woman had acted like she knew something. She'd looked at Clara like she was a clueless fool who wouldn't last a day in this world.

Clara's body moved on autopilot. She pulled up her pants, dropped the coat she'd never bothered to take off, and went to the sink.

She washed her hands and caught sight of herself in the mirror. A pale, hollow-eyed stranger stared back. Her lips trembled before the tears came, and she gripped the porcelain trying to force them back. She splashed cold water on her face and gasped at the sting.

When she straightened, she did a motion she'd made a thousand times at home without thinking. Her hand opened the medicine cabinet.

There they were. Rows of inhalers.

Clara's breath hitched. She closed the cabinet so fast the mirror rattled, cheeks burning with shame at the reflex. Her brain caught up a second later: too many inhalers for one child—ten, maybe more. Neat and plentiful in a world where Sophie had been gasping for air. She opened the cabinet again. Her fingers hesitated, then slipped inside. She pulled out one bottle and froze. The label read: *Andrew Wozniak*. Didn't the woman say she had a daughter? Clara grabbed one more. A different name. The third one had another. Her heart thudded as she scanned the higher shelves. Amoxicillin. Yet another name on the amber plastic.

Clara felt almost detached, like she was watching herself from outside her body. She stood in a room full of medicine that belonged to no one.

Whoever this woman was, these were not her supplies. She must have taken them from others. Maybe from children. Like Sophie.

What could Clara do? Report her to the police? The police station was closed. People had vanished. She didn't know what was happening. This wasn't a time for principles.

Clara pressed both palms to the sink until her knuckles ached. The woman didn't know them. Didn't know where they lived. They would probably never meet again. A dark and desperate whisper resounded in the corner of her mind: If it came down to her daughter or someone else's child there was no choice. There never had been.

*I'm not going to do it. I can't, I can't, I can't,* Clara kept repeating, the words growing louder and louder inside her head.

She stepped back and flushed the toilet again, just in case the woman decided to check on her. She returned to the cabinet, fingers moving quickly as the toilet filled with a loud gurgle behind her, plucking the inhalers one by one and slipping them into her pockets and purse, spreading them out to keep them from clinking together.

Then she stopped. A flicker of guilt cut through the adrenaline. The woman's daughter wasn't Sophie. But she was a child. The woman had a nebulizer, yes. She clearly knew how to manage things. Maybe she had more stashed away. Still. Clara was stealing from a kid.

She pulled one inhaler back out and set it on the shelf.

*She must've stolen them. There's no other way. Who could gather so many otherwise?* And yet … she had never been one to judge other mothers for stealing formula, diapers, anything to keep their babies alive? Survival wasn't a crime. It was instinct. Nature.

*I left her one. She can figure it out. She didn't do that much for us anyway. She wouldn't even sell us one. And she stole them for sure. I'm being more generous than she deserves.*

The words rang hollow in her head. Clara drew a long, shaky breath, forcing her pulse to slow as she tried to pep-talk herself into stepping out.

*She's not going to know. But she'll get suspicious if you stay any longer.*

When she finally dared to open the bathroom door, she felt physically ill—from guilt, from stress, from everything. Her pulse hammered in her ears. She crossed the room in quick strides. Sophie sat on the couch, small and pale, waiting, scared. She was feeling better though also unsettled at being left alone in a stranger's house—Clara guessed by the look in her daughter's eyes—especially after what they'd witnessed at the hospital. Clara bent down, fumbling with her jacket. "Come on, baby. Daddy's looking for us." Her voice shook, but she tried to sound brisk and normal.

She kept her head down, avoiding the woman's eyes as she muttered "thank you" and hurried toward the door.

Fingers brushed her shoulder.

Clara flinched, her heart slamming against her ribs. She spun, certain she'd been caught.

Instead, the woman held out a knobby piece of ginger root. "Here," she said. "I've got too much. You can freeze it."

Clara stared, her face flaming. She forced herself to take it, mumbling yet another strained "thank you." She didn't dare tuck it into her purse and risk being exposed, so she held it awkwardly in one hand while fastening Sophie's buttons with the other.

Clara was about to step away, gently urging Sophie forward while her other hand still gripped the knobby piece of ginger root.

"Mommy?"

The voice made Clara's blood run cold. She turned and saw her: a little girl on the stairs, no older than the ones in the photographs. Blue pajamas dotted with Frozen princesses, exactly like the pair Sophie had once loved until she'd outgrown them.

"I'll be with you in a minute," the woman hushed gently, guiding her daughter back upstairs.

Clara tensed, her whole body coiling inward as if folding into itself. The stolen inhalers pressed on her mind like lead. Her bag and pockets were heavier as though filled with stones weighing her down. She pictured slipping them back, inventing an excuse, faking another wave of nausea just to return what wasn't hers. She imagined the woman finding them gone later, damning her, crying, feeling the despair Clara felt. But Sophie's small, hot hand clutched hers and her mind was made up. There was no turning back. What good would it do?

Besides the woman was clearly resourceful. She'd find another way to save her child, just like Clara had.

It was her daughter's life on the line. The child upstairs might need them too. Or maybe she could do without them. Either way right and wrong no longer existed. The world was gray. It was dull, and cold, and cruel.

She squeezed Sophie's hand tighter.

As they stepped into the cold, Clara thought how unbearable it'd be if that little girl never lived long enough to outgrow her Frozen pajamas. To silence her thoughts (,) she murmured nonsense to Sophie, mostly narrating what was happening.

"We'll go find Daddy. Then we'll go home. You're probably hungry, aren't you? I'll make you something to eat. What would you like?"

"Pizza," Sophie said, "but Mommy?"

"What my love?"

"No pineapple."

They needed to get out of there and fast. Thankfully the car was hidden from the house, and they could slip out of view around the corner. As Clara walked dragging Sophie by the hand, she felt the weight of the woman's gaze on her back and refused to look over her shoulder.

Once they were out of sight, Clara's anxious mind jumped to another problem: David had the car keys. They were stuck.

Snow fell steadily and the sky felt heavier, darker. What time was it? Clara didn't have her phone. They'd left in the morning, around ten. Could the sun already be setting?

"Dang it," Clara muttered under her breath, hoping Sophie didn't hear.

David was already by the car, pacing restlessly. His eyes were wide, breathing rapidly. When he saw them he covered his face in relief. "Where did you go?" he asked, voice trembling.

For the first time, Clara truly saw him worried.

"I'll tell you later," she cut him off, urging him toward the car.

They were almost safe and all Clara wanted was to reach that, whatever *safe* even meant right now.

7

# DAVID

Caleb was waking up when they got home, his face puffy with sleep, dark circles under his eyes from staying up late, reading or whatever it was he'd been doing in his room. The T-shirt he wore was the same one from yesterday, more wrinkled.

"Electricity went out," he announced as soon as they stepped through the door. Only then did David and Clara notice the steady hum of the generator.

David nodded, though there was nothing he could do about it.

"Is it coming back?" Caleb pressed.

"Yes," David said just to stop him.

"Dad …" Caleb called and David turned to face him. Caleb hadn't used "Mom" or "Dad" in a while, speaking instead without names as if to emphasize that they might not be the best parental figures. "Something's wrong, seriously," he said, gripping the back of a chair.

David nodded absentmindedly, hoping Caleb would leave him alone. His mind was crowded, running at full capacity. There was no one to help them here—no relatives, no close friends. His coworkers were gone. No healthcare, no communication, and worst of all very little food. It wasn't just a temporary glitch anymore. Without warning one day everything had simply stopped, and it took them a while to realize it wasn't coming back. It didn't feel like a pause in routine. It felt like the end of it.

They needed to get out. They needed a community; David realized he'd never really had one. Gas was scarce, so driving out was a gamble. But they had to. They needed to get to the airport. Maybe it wasn't too late. Maybe they could board a plane. He tried to push the thought away: At the back of his mind, he couldn't stop thinking that this wasn't like how he'd imagined the world would end.

"Dad, I was serious when I said I want to go to Naya's," Caleb continued, trailing behind him like an annoying fly. "I think we all should. I'm sure they won't mind. They—"

"Caleb," David sighed, closing his eyes in exasperation. "Get dressed. We're going to the airport. Pack light."

Caleb frowned but didn't say a thing, turning and stomping back into his room. David scowled at the heavy thud of footsteps and the slamming of drawers coming from upstairs, then went on to pack as well. Two pairs of underwear, a couple t-shirts, socks, pants. Documents. Very light indeed.

His entire life, ever since he got away from his father, David had worn the mask of conformity. He was allergic to people like him, who got drunk and berated the government while sitting on the comfort of their couch. So David collected labels the way scouts did badges, stitching them together into a neat patchwork of roles and expectations: a student, a father, an employee. For years his only goal had been to wake up each morning, keep his head down, work, contribute, build something, make a difference, no matter how small. Somehow he'd missed out on life itself and on anything genuine. He had nowhere to go, no one to turn to, only people who depended on him and no safety net.

Caleb's plan to go to Naya's village was ridiculous. What could they possibly accomplish there? At best they'd just be more cut off from everything.

The airport wasn't far, but the unplowed streets made the trip much longer. It'd been over a week since the roads were cleared, and the new snowfall had made conditions worse. Driving slowly risked getting stuck, driving fast risked a crash. They passed three wrecks, even though the city was nearly empty. One car had slammed into a street post, abandoned and buried under a layer of snow. Two others had collided, abandoned and empty, their owners vanished as if swallowed by the gray air.

A couple of times the car skidded dangerously, and out of the corner of his eye David saw Clara grab the handle above the door. She always had opinions about his driving and never missed a chance to point out the obvious: you're too close to this car, that guy's merging into our lane, you're driving too fast.

Yet she'd been suspiciously quiet.

In fact she hadn't said a word since the hospital. She wouldn't tell him what had happened. Yes, Sophie had been seriously sick, but she seemed better when he returned. Yes, he had committed a crime—breaking into a hospital, stealing. But the place they'd stormed with the crowd had been completely empty. Whatever expensive equipment or medication had once been there was gone long before they arrived. David managed to find a few packs of ibuprofen and some over-the-counter cold medicine scattered across the floor, but that was it. The hospital had been cleared out with precision, like part of a planned, organized evacuation.

They shouldn't have wasted their time. They should've gone straight to the airport. They should've left the moment he arrived at the base and saw it deserted, an industrial corpse left to rot, frozen and slowly buried under snow.

When they'd come to Fairbanks it was mid-August, and the leaves had already started turning. He thought how beautiful it all looked as the plane descended, their stomachs floating with each dip. It was Sophie's first time flying. Despite their worries she took the flight well, just a little tense during takeoff, but the landing amused her and she giggled at the tickling in her belly.

Caleb sat by the window, half-hidden behind the long fringe his mother could never convince him to cut. But as they began to descend, he leaned closer, peeking out. Their new home.

How deceitful the weather had been, the soft colors and mild air welcoming them with open arms, such a relief after the smoldering Carolina summer, before turning rainy and then bitterly cold. They'd arrived with so much, but it'd felt like almost nothing.

Now each of them carried only a single bag. Sophie, pale and coughing, had her little backpack, bright red and yellow with some cartoon characters on it—David didn't know which ones, though at least it made her easy to spot and that was enough. Caleb had a black backpack that looked ready to burst. David didn't know what he'd packed; a flashlight stuck out of the side pocket, and the bottom was so stretched that he figured Caleb had shoved a sleeping bag in there. The boy slouched awkwardly, likely under its weight, clutching his coat as if his stomach hurt.

David didn't want to admit that he felt a flicker of jealousy. If they ended up stranded somewhere, a sleeping bag would be useful. If not for him or Clara, then for Sophie. But there was no time to dwell on that. They weren't a camping family, and the only sleeping bag in the house belonged to Caleb.

David debated what to do with the car if they managed to catch a flight. Should he leave it somewhere safe, where it wouldn't get broken into or towed, so they could retrieve it once this was all over?

His plans fell through. They couldn't even drive up to the

building. Cars were scattered everywhere, the road to the departures completely blocked. They had to park almost a mile away and abandon the vehicle. David hesitated, wondering if this was a mistake. But they couldn't stay in the city with no connection to the outside world, food and gas running out.

They trudged through deep snow toward the terminal, at least the effort kept them warm.

The first thing David noticed was the darkness. The lights were out. The glass building, usually glowing at this hour, looked hollow and lifeless. His heart sank. Was the airport closed too?

Then it hit him: There wasn't a single plane taking off. They would have seen one by now. He tried to remember if he'd spotted any in the sky over the past few days, but he couldn't. Some things are so constant, so ingrained in memory, that when you try to recall a single instance all you get are echoes of every other time—yesterday, last week, maybe years ago, maybe a lifetime.

When they finally reached the building, there wasn't even a crowd like at the hospital. Just a few people standing around, some already leaving.

David's heart picked up. "Is it closed?"

"Yeah," someone called back, their voice filled with the same hopelessness that seeped through David's mind and body like poison.

He turned to another person. "Are there any planes? Any staff?"

"No. Nobody's inside."

David, who'd been carrying Sophie for the last half mile, handed her to Clara without care, almost absently, and ran to the doors. They were locked. The glass in one of the sliding doors was shattered, proof that others had already tried to get in.

On the other door, a single handwritten note read:

Airport closed.

All flights have been grounded indefinitely.

All staff are to return home and remain off-site until further notice.

There was nothing they could do.

"There are more cars than people," Clara said.

David turned around, ready to snap at her, to tell her to shut up and stop stating useless facts, then noticed she was right. Cars crowded the lot, some buried under heavy snow, others abandoned mid-turn, doors hanging open. Some looked as though they'd been there for days. Somewhere in the distance, a faint metallic groan of wind against metal echoed. His lungs turned to stone as his mind began to recognize the pattern. Too many cars, too few people. They'd left in a hurry—and probably weren't planning on coming back.

"Get inside. Wait there." David gestured toward the broken glass. Inside, the air was cold and stale, but at least they were shielded from the icy gusts.

Cold and shivering, Clara, Caleb, and Sophie obeyed.

David circled the building, fighting the relentless wind that bit through his coat. The runways were enclosed by a tall fence, yet he didn't hesitate. He climbed it and tumbled onto the snow below, his body numb and stiff. For a moment he lay there, letting a dark thought creep in—how peaceful it would be to stay where he was, to freeze in his sleep, painless.

He forced himself up and pushed through the snow to the icy edge of the runway. Not a single plane sat waiting. An unnatural stillness he'd never seen before. Someone had taken all the aircraft, moved everyone out of them, and left the rest behind. To what end?

His foot struck something solid. A suitcase buried in the snow. He stepped over it, felt another thud underfoot. A second suitcase. This one was open, spilling clothes and small belongings onto the snow. Items scattered as if someone had been searching frantically before abandoning everything.

The wind picked up, carrying a hollow whisper across the tarmac. Somewhere far away metal groaned again. David stood still, unsure whether he was waiting or accepting the reality around him, gathering the resolve to move forward, to find new ways, to keep trying.

The cold bit through his coat—snow had worked its way into his shoes when he fell. He was growing colder by the minute, but the discomfort grounded him, stripping his thoughts to the most basic needs: shelter, warmth. He turned and retraced his steps. When he returned, he saw Clara and Caleb locked in a heated argument. Caleb stood rigid, clutching his jacket awkwardly in front of him.

"What's going on?" David asked.

"He broke into the neighbor's house and took that cat!" Clara spat, her voice trembling with fury. "And now he brought it here!"

Caleb's eyes flashed. "She was cold! Hungry! Was I supposed to just let her die?" he shot back, gripping the jacket tighter.

David stepped closer and caught sight of something under the zipper—whiskers, a glint of shiny eyes peeking out.

"Are you out of your mind?" David said flatly.

The cat crouched, tense, ears pinned, yet it seemed to trust Caleb despite the noise.

"Get rid of it!" Clara insisted.

"No! She's going to die here!" Caleb blurted almost crying now, clutching the cat like it was the only thing he could hold on to.

"They won't board us with the cat!" Clara said.

David sighed heavily. "There are no planes."

He looked between them, then the cat, and finally shook his head. "Let's go back to the car." He stepped toward Caleb and added firmly, "You'll put the cat back where you found it and this will be the end of it. I'm not feeding another mouth."

"Should we try the mayor's?" Clara asked quietly. "Maybe he's still there."

David almost rolled his eyes, but stopped himself. "If everyone's gone, he wouldn't be here either."

"Wouldn't hurt to check, would it?" Clara said. "What else are we supposed to do?"

She wasn't wrong. There wasn't much else they could do but go home and stare at each other, pretending everything was fine—until the food ran out, the electricity and heat failed, and they were left to starve and freeze.

They didn't know what was happening, and running blind felt reckless. Driving out of the city in this storm was suicide. There were no gas stations open, no cell service, probably no other drivers. David had just enough fuel to maybe reach Anchorage, then what? What if there was nothing there either?

He gave Clara a quick, sharp nod.

They left the kids at home. Clara gave Caleb quiet instructions on what to do if Sophie got worse, then they headed to the mayors.

David didn't say it in front of the kids, but he was already thinking about stopping by a grocery store on their way back to secure—one way or another—more food. For that he might need help, and his wife, however meek and uncertain she was, was his only option. Caleb might have supported him more, yet he was still a child. David and Clara were adults. They would do what needed to be done.

To David's relief and surprise, the mayor was home. If even one figure of authority remained, maybe not all was lost. A darker voice in his mind whispered that if the mayor had been left behind while everyone else evacuated, perhaps he wasn't much use after all.

The mayor's house was surrounded by cars and people waiting outside, while the man himself tried to hold the crowd back from his porch. Behind him, his wife stood with a gun in her hand and a look of fierce determination. She was in her fifties, fake-blond, fake-tanned, with a camel coat thrown over her shoulders. *Ridiculous*, David thought. She clearly didn't know how to hold or aim the gun properly, but it didn't matter. A 9mm in the wrong hands could still do plenty of damage.

Though David had never liked guns, especially not with kids in the house, watching the mayor's wife hold her ground made him wish he had one too. Not to use. Just to keep close. He'd thought about it before, getting a license, a weapon. Because the worst things always came without warning. Now it was too late for that.

They got out of the car. Clara, pale and drawn under her coat, followed him without a word.

There was something different about her, a shift that had given his once soft, malleable wife a solid core to hold her upright and give her purpose. Where she'd always curved around him and the kids, she seemed to be clinging to that center, learning how to shape herself around it. It felt almost foreign. Alien.

But in this odd new world, she was someone new too.

The mayor, an overweight man in his sixties who looked like someone's kindly grandfather, was speaking to the crowd. David pushed through to listen.

"I'm with you. I understand your frustration. I'm frustrated too. I've gotten no information, and as you can see, I'm still here. I'm not going anywhere. We need to calm down, and I'd like a few people to step forward so we can form a committee and plan our next actions. With all due respect I find it difficult to discuss things fully right now. I'm alone and you are many."

The crowd roared with approval. Two men stepped forward —one short, with a round red face, sweating even in the cold, the other tall and lean with a moustache, about David's age  David felt as if someone had pushed him forward. He thought it was Clara, then realized no one had. He'd advanced on his own.

More men—and a few women—stepped forward. Soon, about forty people had gathered near the front. The mayor surveyed the crush of bodies and began to sift through them, pointing at random. "You, you, and you, sir. Ma'am," he added, nodding at a woman who'd pushed forward and now looked unsure how to decline. David was among the seven people chosen.

Clara stayed behind in the crowd. He looked back to make sure she understood what was happening, but her face was blank.

He hesitated, wondering if he should go back to her. This was their only chance to learn something useful, maybe even get help. They needed others now, especially when everything they'd depended on—the banks, the infrastructure, the hospitals, the food supply—had collapsed. *A person could've survived alone once, maybe, but in the last centuries humankind has grown soft, spoiled by comfort and convenience.*

The small group of people entered the mayor's house to the sounds of singular shouts behind them:

"Hospital's closed!"

"No gas! No food!"

"You must know something!"

The mayor shut the doors, nodding stiffly to the people outside. The polite public mask slipped from his face. The kindly grandpa was gone. His eyes dulled, the corners of his mouth sagged, and the man who'd just played servant of the people turned into someone tired and irritated. His face looked as sour as his wife's. He scanned the group, squinting as if their very presence gave him a headache.

"Right. In here."

His wife stayed by the front door, pistol in hand, watching them track snow over her expensive white carpets with a mix of disdain and … no, when David looked again, it was just disdain. The mayor crossed the hall and opened the door to a smaller room that looked like a home office. A green lamp with a bronze stem glowed dimly on the desk, casting a sickly, worn light. In the corner a globe-shaped bar gleamed with bottles of every size and shape, though none were meant for them. David caught himself thinking he might understand his father a little, drinking to blur the weight of the day.

The mayor sank into his chair, which creaked under his weight, and David and the others gathered closer. He felt like a schoolboy called into the principal's office to be scolded for something he couldn't remember. A small brown leather loveseat sat against the wall, but no one dared to sit without permission.

"Has anyone tried driving out?" the mayor began without preamble. "When was the last time you had contact with anyone outside Fairbanks?"

The volunteers exchanged glances. "A few days ago … maybe a week," mumbled a man in a stiff, grease-stained Carhartt jacket.

David tried to remember when Clara had first told him she couldn't reach her family in North Carolina. Was it last Monday? Or Tuesday?

"Don't you have a private line or something?" another man pressed.

"We do," the mayor admitted. "In the city hall. But everything's dead. Been dead for days. I don't know what to tell you. This has never happened before."

"Has anyone tried the military base?" the woman asked.

"Everyone's gone from the base," David said finally, drawing attention. "And from the hospital. The airport's shut down. It's like they pulled all their staff out."

Selectively. Simultaneously. And left everyone else behind. Everyone who was considered nonessential. *Useless*, David thought to himself.

"Who—*they*?" asked a bearded man in a heavy hunting coat.

"I don't know," David said, "They're gone. All of them."

"Are you in the military?"

"No. But I work at the base," David said, then studied their faces, finally adding, "Any of you?"

The men shook their heads. David thought of their neighbors, Max and Amanda. According to Clara's restless spying, they were gone too. Not a word to them, not a hint—like perhaps they should leave the city, or prepare for what was coming and stock up on food. So much for the friendly fellows who once invited them over for dinner. Hell, they even left the damn cat behind.

"Is there a war or something?" a younger man to David's right asked.

"With whom?" a bearded man shot back.

"Hell if I know. China?" the younger man said, throwing his head back in exasperation.

The mayor raised his voice, forcing authority into the room. "Speculating won't get us far. We need volunteers. We'll send them to Anchorage for help. We'll collect enough gas for them to make it there and back. Regardless of what they find they must return and report. However bad it is."

It sounded reasonable. David nodded, though a tight unease wound through his chest. How bad did the mayor really mean? Deep down he clung to the hope that this was just a mistake, a temporary glitch in the system, something like the 2003 blackout that had plunged half the Northeast into darkness.

"Three volunteers," the mayor said. "If the car gets stuck in the snow three men are more likely to pull it out. Who will go?"

People exchanged nervous glances, waiting for someone else to move first. They'd been eager to talk, to argue, to feel involved—but no one wanted to volunteer.

"My wife's sick. Can't leave her alone," a red-faced man muttered, adjusting his crooked cap.

Another had a herniated disk. Couldn't sit in a car for long.

When the mayor's eyes landed on David, he felt himself shrink. "My daughter's sick," he mumbled. "And my son ..." The rest of the words died in his throat.

The mayor didn't comment. He slapped the table. "Then we need to find someone. How about we talk to the rest of the folks over there?"

He got up, rushing them all to the door.

Volunteers were found. An eager woman, seemingly tall and strong, stepped forward first. Two men followed her.

The mayor explained the task and added graciously, "You can take my Land Rover. It has winter chains on."

David glanced outside, thinking that the Land Rover probably got terrible gas mileage. Since no one else said anything, neither did he.

"Meet back here at two tomorrow and the next day," the mayor said. "We'll share news and plan next steps."

They began collecting gas from whoever had it. Some went to their cars, others protested, demanding a solution right this minute as if snapping their fingers could magically fix everything. David used the moment to quietly edge away, ashamed he'd even stepped forward. He had a family to protect, and their resources were sparse. Clara's car was barely half full. His own tank was low, the arrow on the gauge triggering a spike of anxiety. Every mile he drove would be a risk. No cash, no supply lines, no guarantee of help. At least they had the two canisters.

The last time he'd worried about running out of gas was after he lost his job in North Carolina, but it hadn't felt this dire. Back then there were credit cards. Options to fall back on. Even Clara's mother. And he'd rather face her venom than whatever waited for them now. The unknown.

He returned to the car and found Clara waiting, locked out again. She was trembling under her coat, said nothing. He wanted to ask why she was so quiet, without her usual comments about neighbors, family, or that ugly dog she'd have surely noticed. But he already knew. She was thinking the same he was, and neither of them wanted to say it aloud.

For the first time in years, he felt something close to understanding. He lifted his hand as if to reach for her, then let it drop back to his side.

# 8

# CLARA

The power was back on when they came home, the generator quiet. *Thank God.*

Sophie sat cross-legged by the TV, absorbed in a cartoon on a scratched DVD Caleb must have put on. She was seemingly doing better, even though her cough still rattled through her chest.

Seeing Sophie improve brought Clara relief, bitterly mixed with irritation at Caleb. She'd told him to stay with his sister, to keep an eye on her; clearly her words meant nothing. He'd stopped listening to anyone, a selfish teenager who cared only about his own little world and his friends. Family was supposed to come first. It always had for Clara. Why didn't it matter to anyone else in *her* family?

She stormed into Caleb's room and shoved the door open harder than she meant to. For a split second she thought she should've knocked—there were things mothers weren't supposed to see—but the room was empty. The bed was unmade, dirty socks scattered on the floor, the desk buried under papers and textbooks. Normal.

Except her son was nowhere to be seen.

A faint, acrid smell of cat urine made her grimace, though no cat was in sight. It was either curled up somewhere out of view or had slipped outside.

"Caleb?" Clara called, her voice tight.

No reply.

"Caleb?" Again, quieter, uncertain.

David came up the stairs. "Where is he?"

"I don't know."

They tore through the rooms finding nothing.

"Fuuuck!" David's shout came from the garage.

Clara flinched. He'd never allowed himself to swear, not since they'd had children. The house had been a cuss-free zone. She dashed past Sophie without a glance.

The garage yawned open, overwhelming her with too much empty space. Her car was gone.

David strode back to the living room. "Do you know where Caleb went? Did he say when he's coming back?"

Sophie shook her head.

"You didn't see him leave?"

"I did."

"And you didn't ask where he was going?"

"He didn't say."

David turned toward Clara with an I-will-kill-him look. Clara shut her eyes, exhausted, and turned to the window. Outside, the streetlamps that should have been glowing stood like helpless pillars, leaning into the weight of the darkness.

"He's gone to the village. To *that* girl," she said grimly.

He'd tried to warn them, but they hadn't thought he was serious. He'd taken her car and the last of their gas, leaving them stranded. He'd abandoned his own family. For a girl.

"He took the kitty," Sophie said quietly, coughing through the words.

Clara stared blindly into the empty garage. Her chest felt hollow. Caleb wasn't coming back. Did he even make it there?

What if something happened to him? What if he was lying broken somewhere with no one to call for help? And how would they even know?

She turned to David. He stood frozen, lost in a stupor, staring into the open kitchen cabinet.

"We need to go after him," she said.

David looked at her, then away, then back. "No."

Her voice rose. "What do you mean *no*? He's our son!"

"He left," David said quietly, almost to himself, looking somewhere beyond her. "He made his choice. He didn't want to be here. He's on his own now."

"David no!"

He buried his face in his hands and exhaled through his palms. "What do you want me to say? Going after him is suicide. We don't have enough gas. We're down to one car. It's dark. The roads are murderous. He wants to leave—it's on him."

"This is inhumane!" Clara's voice cracked.

"What's inhumane is walking out on your family. Stealing."

She flinched at the last word, as if it had struck her. She had stolen too—for Sophie.

"What if something happens to him? What if he crashes and no one finds him?" she pressed.

David only shook his head. "Think of Sophie. If we get stuck out there, then what?"

It was the reasonable choice, yet she resented him for saying it so easily. Caleb was his son too. How could he abandon him without a second thought?

She turned toward the stairs.

"Where are you going?" David asked.

"I can't look at you right now," she said through clenched teeth.

She hated him in that moment. Not because he was wrong, but because he was right.

## 9

## CALEB

AT THE AGE OF SEVEN CALEB HAD DECIDED HE MUST'VE BEEN adopted. It was the only explanation that made sense. Somewhere, he told himself, there was a real family, people who'd recognize him as their own instead of studying him with the quiet suspicion reserved for things that don't quite belong, then smiling awkwardly when caught.

From very early in life he could tell when a person was being sincere. He couldn't understand why people were politely fake, and he'd break down when his mother lied about liking a drawing he brought home from school. It was obvious she didn't care for it. Why lie? Why not just tell the truth? Authenticity was something Caleb treasured, though he couldn't have named it back then, and he kept getting into fights with other kids he believed were phony.

He didn't have many friends. In fact, he had only one—a strange boy named Ethan, who used to stand alone during recess before they started hanging out. Ethan was considered "weird."

It wasn't one specific thing that made him an outcast, because every eight-year-old boy had odd quirks. It was the sum of them all. He wore outfits that seemed like they came straight from a church yard sale, chosen by his grandmother. And it could very well be true: He lived with his grandmother and her husband and had never known his parents.

He never cared about football or any other "normal" activities. Another thing the "cooler" kids frowned upon was Ethan's obsession with collecting insects in jars and his ability to name every animal and plant in the area. On top of that, as if trying to be the most unlikeable boy in school, he had a thing for building shelters and learning how to survive in the wild. It was this last obsession that brought him and Caleb together.

Not that Caleb was an outcast too. No, he liked all the same things as his peers and wasn't considered weird. He "dressed well" and was "good-looking." He'd heard Jessie, one of the popular girls, say so. He lived in a "complete family" and checked all the boxes for an eight-year-old to be considered normal.

And yet he chose to be friends with Ethan. One time, after another fight with his usual group of friends, Caleb had been sent to the principal's office for throwing a juice box. It wasn't entirely his fault. Looking back, he knew he shouldn't have thrown it, though Billie was to blame as well. Billie had been describing how he tortured their house cat, and Caleb felt sick to his stomach, full of pity for the animal who sadly died. He called Billie crazy. In response Billie told him to stop being such a *snowflake*.

Caleb wasn't sure what *snowflake* meant. His family never used the word, but he guessed as much—it wasn't a compliment. It was the way Billie said it—all bored and mocking, and then went right back to his story adding even grosser details—that made Caleb snap and fling the juice box he'd been squeezing in his hand at him.

The next day when Caleb walked into the classroom, he saw

Billie's face and knew that if he tried to rejoin the group Billie would make him pay for what had happened, even though it was just a juice carton and no real damage was done. For Billie it was a matter of reputation. Caleb would have to accept that if he wanted to be part of the group again.

For a split second, he considered it and even took an uncertain step toward his friends. Then he went and sat by Ethan, trying to talk to him. Ethan, used to bullying, was at first closed off and unresponsive. He eventually opened up. Within a few days, Caleb realized that he and Ethan had far more in common than he did with any of the other boys. Social status was a small price to pay for being true to himself.

And so they became friends.

Another odd thing about Ethan that no one else knew was his obsession with running away. Every so often they would play pretend, disappearing for a few hours as if they were gone for good. Caleb soon realized Ethan was serious about doing it one day. He was saving money. He had a hiding spot in the woods. He prepared food, dried bread, snuck chocolates, and had even found a rusty hatchet to hide there. Together they learned to set traps for animals, in case they ever needed to hunt for real, living off the grid with no one to answer to and no one to feed them. Caleb was thrilled and gladly played along. He never thought he'd actually run, but he enjoyed imagining it: hunting, chopping wood, making fire. No parents. No school. Freedom.

Ethan's grandmother's husband was a truck driver. On the weekends he was home he'd take Ethan camping. And though Ethan loved being in the woods and knew everything about making fires, building shelters, setting traps for animals, and identifying edible plants, for some reason he hated going with his step-granddad.

One day, when they were twelve, Ethan didn't come to school. The phone at his house wouldn't answer, and when Caleb tried to walk by, he was spooked away by a police car parked at the entrance.

At home his parents told him Ethan had moved away to live with family in Alaska. At school Caleb quickly learned a different story. Rumors spread about what had really happened to Ethan, that he'd run away one night and, while trying to stop a car in the dark, been hit by it. There were more rumors about why he'd run too.

Caleb didn't know what to think. He didn't want to believe any of it, but he still felt guilty for not noticing the signs. He also wished Ethan had told him he was going to run. Maybe, if Caleb had gone with him, they would be safe somewhere in the woods, warm in a shelter, near a fire they'd built.

That evening Caleb went into the woods to check on their hiding place. Everything was still there: the hatchet, the candy, the bread. Rain had gotten inside the plastic, turning the food supplies into a pulpy mess alive with maggots. *Fly larvae*, Ethan would have corrected him.

Caleb tried telling his parents about the camping trips Ethan hated, they refused to listen. Soon after they'd stopped talking about it altogether, consumed by his little sister's health, and made it clear that Caleb was expected to move on as well.

He wiped the tears away angrily with the back of his hand before gripping the steering wheel again. The roads were terrible, and he did his best to steer through the gathering gloom. The sedan slid too easily on the ice, its tires useless against the rutted snow. A few times he nearly got stuck, but he pushed through, pressing the gas pedal. His worst fear was stalling out, trapped between drifts with no way forward and no way back.

His second biggest fear was that the village wouldn't welcome him, refuse to let him stay. When he'd met them before, they'd been wary of him—he understood why. Naya was dating a white boy. He wished he could show them he knew how to hunt and survive, at least in theory, but the conversation never went that way. They were curt and polite, exchanging a few phrases in a language he didn't understand. He later asked Naya to teach him some; she was reluctant.

At times it felt as though they were drawn together because she was moving toward his way of life, and he toward hers, meeting somewhere in the middle. However, that same pull was sending them off in different directions, and little by little, they were growing apart.

He pushed those thoughts away.

They would surely let him in. They were good people after all, and they knew him. Besides he wasn't coming empty-handed. He had brought supplies. Not much, but at least something. He hated taking from his own family, though he saw no other choice.

And he knew things. He was ready to work, to work hard. Physical labor didn't scare him. If he couldn't be exceptional, he could at least make sure he wasn't a burden.

They would take him in. Maybe later they could find his parents and Sophie, save them. Then they'd see him differently. They would finally listen. And if not he'd at least insist on taking Sophie.

Tears welled up in his eyes again.

He tried to focus on Naya instead, on what tomorrow might bring, and whether tomorrow would even come. Anything to keep his mind off Sophie, wide-eyed and clutching her blanket, watching him gather his things and hesitantly take some of the food his parents had brought home *that day*. The day it all started. His parents had come to pick him up from a school that had descended into chaos, with no teachers in sight. The few who had shown up and hadn't immediately left to pick up their own kids had locked themselves in the teachers' lounge for an "emergency meeting," leaving the teenagers to their own devices. The kids wandered the halls, sharing conspiracy theories and vapes, laughing and cracking jokes. No reason to panic. If everything fell apart, there was nothing to be done. If things were fixed and returned to normal, there was even less reason to worry.

He thought of Ethan too. How he would be calm and serious, telling him what they needed to survive, making lists and plans out loud. Ethan had sparked in him a love for the idea of living a smaller but fuller life. Having met Naya, he felt like she came from a world that understood him better than the one he was born into.

Sophie's faint voice pierced his thoughts, asking where he was going as he rushed through the house packing. He pretended not to hear. He couldn't bear to tell her he was leaving them. Really leaving.

He wondered if walking away from her had been a mistake. No. It was the right thing to do. If anything happened to Sophie while she was with him, he'd never be able to live with himself. Mom had all her medication and knew everything about her care. She'd have to come with them, but there was no time to argue or persuade. They never listened.

Even though Caleb had always felt like he didn't belong in his own family when Sophie was born, sick and fragile, he faded into the background. He never felt envy or jealousy toward her. On the contrary, she was the daughter their parents wanted and needed, accepting their care with gratitude. He didn't need them and they resented him for that, but Sophie gladly took all the attention and affection. Strangely that made things easier for Caleb, because his parents finally stopped trying to get him to fit in and be social. Caleb slipped to the edges of the family without a fight.

Freedom came in small doses: Afternoons when Mom was at yet another doctor's appointment and he could make himself a

PB&J, sprawl in front of the TV, and forget the world until someone came home to scold him. He could have Ethan over, though his parents didn't love that friendship. They would play video games or watch survival shows, making plans about how they'd do it and mocking the people who failed and got eliminated.

After Ethan was gone, Caleb became even more fixated on wilderness survival. He watched every video he could find, learning how to light a fire in the rain and build a shelter from scraps. He asked his parents to sign him up for a hunting club and get him a gun; they flatly refused. Frustrated he promised himself he'd do it the day he turned eighteen.

Whenever snow fell, he tried to build igloos in the park, shivering inside them, trying to imagine what it would be like to live in one. In summer he dragged long branches home and hid them under the porch, stockpiling for a wigwam. When his parents discovered the pile during spring cleaning, they made him explain himself, then clear out the space and get rid of "the fire hazard."

His parents never asked his opinion about moving to Alaska. He tried to object but they shut him down immediately, calling him selfish and insisting he didn't understand the situation. He did understand, though to him it was a matter of want, not need. His father wanted to move, so they were moving. He knew they had money problems. He knew his father couldn't stand his grandmother, and she couldn't stand him. They never explained any of it to their kids. They just told Caleb to pack, and that was it.

The assumption was that he would graduate and go to college somewhere in North Carolina, giving his mother an excuse to move them back. Yet Caleb thought college was nonsense—a money grab, a Ponzi scheme. His father had a degree, and for what? Still buried in student debt, scraping by on his salary. Caleb didn't want that life. He kept it to himself, knowing arguing would be pointless. He had his own plan: to work hard every day after school and through the summers, save up money, and, when the time was right and he was old enough, follow his dream. He would buy a sleeper and move closer to the wilderness, venturing further and deeper until he was somewhere no one could find him.

They moved and Caleb found that he suddenly loved it here, something his mother seemed to resent even more. Once during an argument, she exhaled, "Why couldn't you find friends in North Carolina?" He knew exactly what she meant: white friends. Someone she would approve of.

Alaska agreed with him, with its short summers and harsh winters, though he'd experienced one of each so far. It only took to people who valued freedom and self-reliance.

Then he met Naya. They went to the same school, along with two other kids from her village. He noticed her the way he'd noticed Ethan. She wasn't exactly an outcast and got along with everyone, but there was something slightly distant about her, as if her world was just a little out of sync with the one everyone else at school lived in.

Though he'd been the one to notice her, Naya was the one who took the initiative speaking to him first, and suddenly he, someone who always preferred to stay silent and keep his distance, was talking nonstop. For most of the time they became that—talking buddies. Friends even. She never laughed at his speeches about living off the grid. He tried to hold himself back, but with her the words slipped out before he could stop them. She listened.

It took him three months to work up the courage to ask if she wanted to go out. She said yes.

They didn't go to a coffee shop after school or to the arcade where most kids hung out. No. Instead she took him to the edge of the park, past the cleared paths and into the trees. There, she showed him animal tracks in the snow and how to tell which way the wind had blown the night before. Her uncle was a deer hunter, she explained, and she had learned a lot from him. She pointed out plants, explaining what was edible, what could be used as medicine, and what could kill you if you weren't careful. Caleb realized how little he actually knew, though he was eager to learn. He'd never met anyone his age, besides Ethan, who understood the land so well, and it felt like stepping into a hidden world—a world that belonged to her and now maybe a little to him too.

Suddenly his determination to be alone faded; he knew he wanted to be with Naya always. He also knew his family would never approve of her, would never accept her, which only made him like her more. The way they asked about her made him furious. It wasn't simple curiosity about his new friend. They didn't really care about her as long as she was "safe to hang out with" or came from a "good family" and didn't have any bad habits. Their questions carried something else, bordering on prejudice. He sensed deep down they felt superior to Naya and her people, though they never said it outright. How could they, people so disabled by civilization, think they were better than anyone? What kind of delusion was that? Where did it come from?

True superiority came from independence and self-sufficiency. If you could survive when the familiar world fell away, then you were superior. It wasn't about beating someone else—it was natural selection. Those with skill, knowledge, stamina, and perseverance would endure. His parents had none of that. Sure, his father claimed he did everything for the family, but did he really? He worked hard for them, yes, but once the familiar patterns were gone, so was his footing. His mother liked to seem refined and cosmopolitan, yet ultimately, she was nothing more than an ordinary housewife who built herself up on the backs of others. Somehow, they still acted as if they were too good for Naya.

Of course, it stayed beneath the surface. His mother even invited Naya for dinner once. Caleb sensed it wasn't out of hospitality. It was surveillance, an excuse to size her up, to place her neatly in the hierarchy they carried in their heads. It didn't escape him how his mother's gaze lingered on Naya's hand-made, intricately embroidered handbag, then slid to her beaded bracelets and hand-crafted jewelry. Naya never said anything—not at dinner, not afterward. When he tried to apologize , she only shrugged, as if it wasn't a big deal. Maybe to her it wasn't. She was above all that.

Days before it all started, Naya had been strange, quiet and reserved. When he asked her about it, she couldn't explain. She only said that something felt heavy in her mind, like a storm was coming, and nothing more. Later, she mentioned that someone in the village had dreamed of a dark cloud rising and swallowing the world.

He brushed it off then, but she hadn't sounded delirious or crazy. She spoke calmly, almost matter-of-factly, as if to say, *I'm just telling you. Do with this information what you will.* Like his father, who never trusted anything his mother said, Caleb had acted the same way and he felt guilty for it.

However, something in her tone, in her composure, unsettled him. Maybe he was imagining it but he felt it too, that subtle change in the air, as if the temperature had dropped by a few degrees, as if a faint draft had slipped past his ankles. Intangible things are hard to believe until they become tangible. By the time they do, it's too late.

She missed a few days of school after that, and he couldn't get a hold of her. The last time he saw her was the day it all started. She'd told him he should come to the village. He should have gone with her then.

· · ·

The cat meowed from his gym bag. He had to put her there so she wouldn't run around the car, get spooked, cause them to crash.

"We'll be there soon, Cat." His voice came out low and broken, like he was sick. He'd thought about giving her a proper name, but she probably already had one she was used to. It felt wrong to change it, so he kept calling her Cat.

Something was happening, and it was happening fast. His parents weren't reacting quickly enough. Yes, they were worried and anxious, and they'd gathered some food, but it wasn't nearly enough. He'd tried to warn them, tried to tell them. Did they listen? No. As always,  they silenced him and did what they thought was right. He already knew there were no flights when they went to the airport. Naya had told him there hadn't been planes in the sky for days.

He shouldn't feel bad about leaving them. It was a matter of survival. He had to choose between staying with his parents and little sister and running out of food or saving himself. And as much as it hurt, as much as he still loved them, he knew he had to go.

He tried not to think about what would happen to his family. The thoughts made his eyes water again, made him want to turn back, to beg them to come with him. Though it was useless. The more desperate he sounded, the more annoyed they would be. So he kept driving.

Naya had once explained that when you leave your bubble willingly, it's best to consider yourself dead. You take your life out of the hands of others and into your own. For those you leave behind you are as good as gone.

He tried to imagine what it would feel like for his family to treat him as if he were dead. The thought was brutal. He'd never meant to cause them that kind of pain.

Caleb wished his cellphone worked. He kept it with him anyway, a useless relic of his old life. He wished he could call

Naya and talk to her as he drove, to keep his thoughts from circling back to the same dark places. He wished he could call his parents and explain everything. He wished they would understand him and let him go.

The cat meowed from the back seat, probably uncomfortable. But her mewing made him feel just a little better. He wasn't completely alone.

10

# DAVID

They had so little food—barely to last them two weeks. Perhaps a little longer if they rationed. Almost no gas, certainly not enough to make it to Anchorage and back in this weather. The electricity had come back after a long blackout and the water was running too, which was a relief, though he didn't expect either to last. The streetlights never returned and that bothered him. The world was falling apart. It was clear that the military and the medical staff had been evacuated. But how? And where? And how come nobody, literally no one, knew what was going on?

He grabbed his cellphone out of habit yet again, then flung it aside, angrier each time. A useless piece of plastic. Another irrelevant thing.

Nothing mattered. They'd worried about savings dwindling against the growing credit card debt, about how low their 401(k) accounts were, about how unfair the world was to people who tried to preserve it for future generations. None of that had any weight anymore.

Then there was Caleb. Whatever they'd thought was just teenage angst had turned into his running off. He had abandoned his family. He had stolen from them. He stole the car, the gas, the supplies. He did something David was afraid to admit he'd thought about, but of course never acted on it. It was unfathomable, leaving his family, Clara and the kids, and venturing off to build a new life somewhere else, with someone else.

He'd never leave his family, no matter how much Clara and her mom got on his nerves, no matter how exhausting fatherhood had become.

When Caleb was twelve, right after his friend had died, he'd stolen David's pocketknife and disappeared into the woods to cut branches for one of his makeshift shelters. He sliced himself badly, deep enough that the bleeding wouldn't stop. Clara spotted it at dinner, blood soaking through his sleeve. The ER had to give him nine stitches. He never admitted how bad it was, never said a word. He lost the knife, too, stumbling back home. David shouted at him for running off, for stealing, for hurting himself, for hiding it. But what hurt most was the knife. It was the only thing he had from his father. He didn't even remember how it ended up with him when he left home, only that it did, and he'd kept it sharp all those years. Not used it. Just kept it. Losing it had felt like losing a piece of himself.

It was happening again. Caleb had stolen something from him and run away without a word. Deep down David feared the same ending—that the boy would come back empty-handed, covered in blood. Or worse.

He forced the thought away. No. Caleb was grown now. He'd made his choice, turned his back on them. He was on his own, as David had once been when he walked away from his father, cutting all ties.


When David was sixteen his mother was already gone, and he'd been counting the days until he was legally an adult so he could leave. That day his father, as usual, came home drunk. He wasn't the quiet kind of drunk; he was the kind who barged into David's room to pick a fight. They'd never had a warm father-son relationship, but after David started growing up and his mother died, his father began treating him like an inconvenience—someone he resented but had to tolerate.

"Show me you're a real man!" he barked, finding David with his books. "When I was your age I-I was working at the factory. And you? You're a waste of s-space."

It was the same line David had heard since he was twelve. He wasn't even sure when his father had started at the factory, only that he'd been stuck there ever since, no prospects, no growth. It seemed all he wanted was to drag David into the same dead life. David wanted out—out of that house, out of the state, away from him. At times, he looked at the shanty town that grew like mushrooms after the rain behind the grocery store and seriously considered joining them one day. What had stopped him had been common sense and one homeless man who'd told him, while he'd been waiting for his father by that same grocery store, unable to leave like a dog tied to a fence, that once you went homeless it's really hard to get back to anything else. That it's not just about money or documents, it's about mindset.

David tried to ignore him, thinking that if he didn't react and simply stared at his father's red face and sweat-stained shirt, the man would lose interest and leave him alone. His father kept going, slurred words pouring out like dirty water. "Youu're a p-piece of shiit, that's w-who you aare. Shouuld've made her a-abort youu. But that sstupid bitch refuused."

David's mother had been far from perfect, though his memories of her weren't all bad. Sometimes she yelled, sometimes she slapped, yet she loved him. She cared for him when he was sick. Once she'd taken him to an amusement park with money she'd hidden away from groceries. They had enough for one ride and one hot dog, and he begged her to go on the

Ferris wheel with him. The smell of kettle corn and cotton candy made his mouth water, but he wanted her there more than the treats. When you do something and have nobody to share the moment with, is it really worth doing? His mother was scared of heights, as he came to learn later, but she went with him. She'd gripped the railing so hard her knuckles had gone white and kept telling him to be careful when he leaned outward to see the world from above.

She was no stupid bitch, and he wouldn't let anyone call her that, especially not his father.

Before he could think he was off the bed, swinging his algebra textbook as hard as he could. He struck his father again and again. His father still managed to hit back—once on the cheekbone, once across the jaw—before collapsing. David stood above him, body trembling with rage, raised his foot to kick while his father shivered on the floor. But he stopped. He stopped.

He froze, his mind panicking, trying to decide what to do next when there was nothing to do and no way back.

Then David stormed out, angry tears burning his eyes, making the world blurry and soft. He walked to town in the dark along the highway. It took him two hours to get there on foot. He spent the night on a bench in the park, hoping the police wouldn't find him and bring him back to his father, now even angrier. He didn't know what else to do and went to school the next day. Afterward, he stayed at his friend Matt's house for a few nights until Matt's parents told him he had to go back. They said his father was probably worried and looking for him.

He wasn't. When David returned, prepared for another beating, his father glanced at him, grunted, and passed out in front of the old TV. They never spoke of it again. Nothing like it happened after.

A year and a half later, as soon as he could, David had left. And never came back.

. . .

The mayor's house had become the last beacon of hope, the place people flocked to because there was nowhere else to turn. Desperate and restless they clung to the one remaining figure of authority, the man who might tell them what to do, who might speak for them, though what that meant was uncertain.

David drove there alone, leaving Clara and Sophie at home. Clara hadn't spoken to him since Caleb had left. Maybe even before then. Sophie seemed a little better, but Clara's face had gone pale, drained of feeling, like she was made of stone. She kept looking out the kitchen window that faced the street, carefully, as if afraid someone might see her from outside. David no longer bothered asking what was wrong.

By the time he arrived—fifteen minutes early—a crowd had already gathered outside the house. The mayor stood on the porch, addressing them. His wife wasn't beside him this time, though David caught a glimpse of her face in the window. She noticed him staring and yanked the curtain shut.

"… no news yet. They haven't come back."

David's heart sank. The people they'd sent to Anchorage …

"They should have! It's been more than twenty-four hours," someone shouted.

The mayor lifted his hands. "I'm telling you only what I know. No one has returned. We need to give it another day."

"Send another car! Maybe they're stuck!"

"They're not stuck. It's a Land Rover," the mayor said as if he'd given them a tank. "It has chains. I'm not wasting gas. We'll wait another day."

The crowd reluctantly dispersed, disappointed and dissatisfied. The mayor looked worn out, dark hollows under his eyes, skin sagging as if even his flesh were tired. Even the bald patches on his head seemed larger.

His power was thin. It looked like he was trying to balance

being an authority figure with being the one everyone blamed. An angry mob could do real damage.

David understood that, but he couldn't stop his own anger and frustration. What a waste of gas this trip had been. How could he have known there would be no news? The mayor offered no answers. Why take on a role you couldn't handle?

The strangest part was how much people still trusted elected officials, believing these suits knew what to do when the world was falling apart. They didn't. None of them had any real clue. The mayor was a function, a hollow shell, clinging to power while everything around him crumbled. These people took their offices for themselves, for ambition, for the illusion of control—not to protect anyone. And when people needed them most they were nowhere.

David got home to Clara's worried pacing.

"Electricity is out again."

He knew the lights would fail eventually and never come back. He just hoped this wasn't that moment. Maybe they should start stacking firewood for a house without a fireplace. But how do you build a fire to keep warm without choking on the smoke? Maybe they should do something—anything—instead of sitting and waiting for the dark and the unknown to swallow them. Yet David couldn't bring himself to care. The thought alone was too heavy. He felt moving on habit more than will, so drained that even survival faded into the background.

"How's Sophie?" he asked sinking onto a stool by the counter.

He couldn't remember the last time he hadn't felt tired. Was it age? Was this what getting old felt like? He wasn't that old. Could be just life. When young you wonder why adults always seem frantic, always rushing, always worried. To a teenager, problems look simple: take them one at a time. Money is only paper. You'll earn more, live today.

And then one day, you stop focusing on the now and start

living in the *what's next*. The problems don't wait in line, they pile up. Some you manage, others you don't. It's like living in a house full of sharp-cornered furniture. You keep bruising yourself, and as you memorize where everything is someone rearranges the room and throws in more obstacles. You're always limping, always on guard, always waiting for the next blow.

"She's managing. But she needs a doctor, David," Clara said as if the solution rested entirely on him.

"I know."

11

# DAVID



By the time David arrived there the next day, the crowd that had circled his house had given up and stormed inside. The doors were gaping open, most windows shattered, the cold air coming in. David followed them to find nothing. Everything was already going. Clothes, a little food, the last car, and a few canisters of gas. Whatever the mayor left behind was being snatched up in minutes.

He should have been here sooner. He should have been more insistent, more relentless. Angrier. He shouldn't have left at all. He should have stepped up and organized people. He should have gone to Anchorage with them.

That was the tragedy of David's life: always just a step late, always slightly off the mark. Never quite where he needed to be, never quite enough.

He stood alone. The society he had served was gone. The framework he'd spent his whole life fitting himself into had collapsed overnight, leaving nothing to lean on.

The road not taken had become the only road left, and it led nowhere.

.   .   .

As the primary decision-maker for his family, David was used to being in control. Yet how he wished there were someone to tell him what to do, someone he could surrender to in quiet, grateful acquiescence.

It would've been easier if he were alone, without Clara or Sophie. A thought brushed against his mind. He had the car. He could just ...

No. He glanced around, ashamed as if someone might have overheard him. The floor was empty. He was alone. A crack of breaking glass came from downstairs. Others were scavenging too, tearing through the remnants of someone else's life.

His eyes settled on an antique vase in the corner. Who even had money right now for such things? Expensive. Impractical. A fragile ornament in a world that had no use for decorations anymore.

He picked it up, felt the cool surface, traced the intricate carvings. The last beautiful thing in this world. Then he hurled it against the wall. The vase exploded into a thousand shards, the echo crashing through the rooms.

This world didn't deserve beautiful and useless things.


After leaving the mayor's house David navigated the treacherous streets, the frozen snow turning every corner into a gamble. He didn't care about the danger. His focus was on the store ahead, the one place where he might still find something to feed his family. His determination felt feverish, almost desperate, the kind that burns out whatever strength there's left. Those quiet, shameful thoughts of leaving them behind still clung to him, their guilt eating at him even though he'd never acted on them. He was too tired to think straight, too worn down to hope, yet some dull instinct kept him moving. The least he could do was bring back food.

The fact that he had no money didn't bother him. What was money, anyway? A meaningless concept in a world that had lost all sense of civility. Loans, stocks, savings accounts—all worthless without the framework of society to support them. David's 401(k), his brokerage account, his carefully curated financial security blanket was all rendered obsolete in an instant. He was beyond worrying about those things.

He pulled up to the store and sat in the turned-off car for a while, trying to calm down and convince himself to go through with it.

*Come on. You can do it. Others do it.*

He couldn't. As soon as he reached the store he saw the windows shattered and the door hanging crookedly on its hinges, like at the mayor's house. Inside it was a desolate wasteland. Shelves lay bare, their contents looted by whoever had come before him. David's eyes scanned the empty space, his gaze falling on a ripped bag of rice. He almost kicked it in despair, instead grabbed a plastic bag and began collecting the grains from the floor.


With an unsteady gait he returned to his car and sat down, hands on the wheel, the engine still off. His body shook with convulsive sobs, his face twisted in a silent scream, teeth clenched. The sound that escaped him was terrifying—a low, guttural moan that seemed to rise from the depths of his soul.

He wasn't going to save anyone. He was never going to make them rich or proud or anything else. Their entire life had been survival after survival, and now there wasn't even going to be a future for them. He had failed. He couldn't take care of his family.

He'd cried through the entire drive, emptying himself until

numbness settled in. As he turned onto his street and the rows of dark houses loomed ahead like a line of graves, he wiped his face with the end of his scarf and tried to steady himself, making sure he could walk inside without breaking down and telling his wife he had achieved nothing, that there might be no hope left.

Clara sat in the living room, her face blank, eyes fixed on the dark screen of the TV. She wore her coat, and from the shape of it, he could tell she had a couple of sweaters underneath. The air inside was colder than he liked—not unbearable, but far from comfortable. His legs felt weak.

"Is the heat off?" he asked quietly, hoping she wouldn't notice the tremor in his voice.

"I turned it off to save fuel," she said in a colorless voice. "You can turn it back on, the power's back."

He wanted to tell her it would cost more fuel to reheat the house than to leave it cold, though the words felt pointless. What did it matter? A day sooner or a day later the diesel would run out. The electricity would fail again, the generator would sputter and die, and they'd be left with nothing. He felt too tired to even resent it, too drained to think past the next breath.

Clara's gaze remained fixed ahead. For a moment he wondered if she'd snapped, trapped in a trance, her mind unable to cope. Then she blinked and turned toward him, eyes still empty.

"We need to leave," he said, voice firm but gentle. "We have to go to Anchorage."

Clara's eyes drifted away, unfocused as they often did lately. David held his breath, waiting for a response. Eternity seemed to stretch in agony before she quietly, decisively said, "No."

# 12

# SOPHIE

Sophie didn't think her parents realized she was growing up. That she could hear and understand them, read their faces, and tell when they were forcing a smile while looking at her or the drawings she brought from school. She even tested them once. She took a terrible doodle from a younger kid's accomplishments wall and brought it home, pretending it was hers. Her parents only gave her compliments.

She'd tried to tell her mom she was big enough to do many things on her own, like her homework, and using the nebulizer or the inhaler. Her mom didn't want to see it. Her mom wanted Sophie to stay little. Sophie could tell. So she played along even when she didn't want to. After all, being the little one came with perks. She could skip school whenever she said she wasn't feeling well. She got a phone while most of her classmates didn't even dream of having one. She got to watch cartoons every time she used the nebulizer; sometimes she even asked for it, pretending she felt worse than she really did. Her mom was sure the machine scared her, so she always turned on something cheerful to keep her distracted.

Now everything was different, and her parents simulating

everything was fine made her even more scared. They didn't tell her what was happening, but she could see it in the empty streets, the quiet stores, the way people moved.

It started small. One day she came home from school and Mom looked worried and upset, though she wouldn't say what had happened. Sophie was expected to stay quiet, not ask questions, sit there like one of her dolls and watch her mother fall apart—eyes red, hands trembling—without reacting.

And Sophie didn't. She held it in as much as she could and only cried at night, buried under her blanket. If she cried in front of Mom, it would only make everything worse.

She tried to hide her cough, tried to breathe through her sore throat that felt tighter every day. It reminded her of one of those rubber squeaky toys with a valve. You squeeze it and the air struggles to get through, coming out in a slow, strained wheeze.

Her brother Caleb used to babysit her, even though she didn't really need it back in North Carolina. He didn't pay much attention to her, so she could do whatever she wanted as long as she wasn't too loud. He even let her watch movies that their parents said she was too young for. Scary ones. One time he'd played a movie about the end of the world. He didn't care if she watched. Aliens were crawling out from underground, killing people, destroying cities. Sophie got scared and Caleb told her that sort of thing couldn't happen. He said, though, that the world was coming to an end, just not because of aliens but because of global warming. He explained that slowly, over many years, the Earth would get so hot that people wouldn't be able to grow food or survive and humans would eventually go extinct.

This terrified her, yet she didn't dare tell her parents. If they yelled at Caleb, which they often did, he'd never let her watch another grown-up movie with him. Still, from that day on, she'd been sure the world was going to end—at least as much as she could understand what that meant. Now, she thought, that time had come. Somehow it wasn't like Caleb had said. It wasn't hot, and the world didn't turn into a big desert. It was cold and dark and her parents were scared.

Two days ago, Sophie had watched them rush around, getting ready for whatever was coming. One of the things they did was fill every jar they had with water, the steady sound of the faucet echoing through the kitchen. Her mom carefully positioned jar after jar under the stream, while her dad twisted the lids tight. The jars came in every shape and size, from tiny jam jars to big pickle jars, each one cleaned and filled to the very top. It was kind of interesting, like a school project.

They reassured her that everything was going to be okay, that this was just a precaution. "Do you remember when we read about tornadoes and how people prepare for them? This is kind of like that!" her mom had said, her voice a little too cheerful.

The strangest part, besides the obvious, was that not much had changed. Mom still cooked dinners, and Sophie still watched cartoons. Only there was no school, which she didn't miss at all. She'd already skipped so many days that she hadn't made any friends. And when she tried to approach the other kids, she always felt out of place. During recess, they ran and shouted and played. She tried joining once, but it didn't go well. Her chest tightened, her breathing turned shallow, and though her inhaler worked fine, the school had still called her mom, who'd shown up in a panic, scooped Sophie up, and rushed her to the doctor. No, she didn't miss school. The noise, the chaos of it.

Mom was crying a lot nowadays, especially when she thought Sophie couldn't hear. Every time Sophie approached her and asked what was wrong, her mom's response was always the same: "Everything's fine, baby."

Ever since her mom stole the medicine for her. Stole it from that nice lady and her daughter. Sophie knew it. She'd seen how worried her mom had been when they'd run out. And then, after the woman had refused to sell them more inhalers, her mother had come back from the bathroom hurried, distracted, urging

Sophie to leave. Next thing she knew, they magically had inhalers again. What Sophie didn't know was how to feel about it. It was complicated. *Adult things*. At first she'd been scared her mom had done something bad and could go to prison. But three days had passed and everything stayed quiet. The fear had morphed into shame for what her mom had done. In school they'd talked about stealing and how it was wrong, even if you needed something, because you were always taking away from someone. Sophie knew it was true. Sure, she needed her inhalers. She still couldn't stop thinking that somewhere out there, someone else might be gasping for air because of her. The guilt burned so hot it made her angry.

She sat on the bed, her breathing tight, her chest gurgling like a clogged drain. She knew she needed to use an inhaler. Her eyes landed on it, sitting on her desk where she'd left it. Someone else's name was written on it. Slowly, she got up and walked over. She grabbed it, but instead of bringing it to her mouth, she kept it in her hand and tiptoed down the hall to the bathroom so no one would notice.

There was only one bathroom in the house, everyone had to share it. Right now, it was empty. Sophie quietly locked the door behind her. She opened the toilet and sprayed the inhaler she was holding into it. Then she went to the cabinet above the sink. This was where her mom kept the rest she'd taken. Sophie took them one by one and emptied each into the toilet, then carefully put them back in place. If that little girl didn't get them, neither should her.

It felt right. Fair.

Sophie went back to her room, set the empty inhaler on her desk, and lay down trying to breathe through the tightness in her chest. She knew she had to.

Another thing Sophie knew was that her mom and dad didn't like each other, and together they didn't like Caleb much either. After he'd left—and taken the gas canisters from the garage and some food—Mom and Dad had reached a whole new level of dislike. It was like they couldn't even stand being in the same room or looking at each other. Her mom would always try to talk to her when Dad walked in, as if Sophie was only there to distract her.

Tonight, as Sophie peeked through the railings, they were downstairs standing close, almost touching, like they might hug. That, more than anything, made her feel weird. She'd never seen them hug before.

Her parents' voices were hushed, strained, the kind of whisper that sounded like shouting.

"We have to go, Clara. We can't stay here anymore," her dad said.

"But what about Caleb?" her mom's voice quavered. "What if he comes back and we're not here?"

"He's not coming back," her father said.

*Caleb's not coming back?*

Their voices dropped again, and Sophie couldn't catch what they said next. Then—

"No," her mother said, louder than she probably meant to. "We don't know what's there. What if we get stranded?"

"We'll be fine," her father said. "It's not that far. We have enough gas."

"What if it's the same there? Or worse? Oh my God what if it's worse?" she said, panicking at her own words.

"We'll figure it out. There must be people. Someone will help us. We just need to get to a bigger city."

"What about Sophie? She's too sick. We can't risk it."

They fell silent. Her mom took a step back from Dad and slowly shook her head. "I'm staying with her. We're not going."

Her dad sighed and said, like a verdict, "Then I'll go alone."

Mom stepped further back.

"You've been meaning to abandon this family from day one. From the moment Caleb was born," she hissed.

"What are you talking about?" her father snapped, using his normal voice.

"Admit it. All you want is to run from us."

"That's not true. I'm trying to save us."

"*I*"—her mother pointed to her own chest—"am trying to save our daughter. *I* stole for her. From another child. And *you*'re running around achieving nothing."

"What else do you want me to do, Clara?"

"Just wait it out! Help will come!"

"It won't."

Silence again.

Longer this time.

"Then go," she said finally. "Leave us here. If you don't come back,  I'll know I was right."

"We won't survive if I stay. We'll have a chance if I go."

"Daddy don't go!" Sophie tried to scream from upstairs, but her voice betrayed her. It came out cracked and rough, like a cartoon pirate. She ran downstairs and threw her arms around him, crying, her grief too big for her small body. If Daddy left, what would she do alone with Mom?

Her mom gripped her shoulders, trying to pull her away from him, and said, "Daddy isn't going anywhere."

Dad echoed, "I'm right here," closing his arms around her.


Sophie fell asleep late, still upset, crying, exhausted from her tears. She missed Caleb, and she cried for him too. It was the first time she remembered crying so desperately in front of her parents. Something inside her broke like a dam, and the tears ran nonstop. While she cried both her parents stayed with her, and that made her feel a little safe. She wished it could stay like that forever.

When she woke the room was still dark, everything felt too warm, too tight. She wasn't alone in bed. Her mother was next to her, snoring quietly, her body smelling like stress and sweat and sleep that comes after crying.

*Where's Dad?*

Sophie got up carefully so she wouldn't wake her and padded barefoot to her parents' bedroom. The bed was still made. Her mom always made every bed, clinging to that routine. Except Caleb's. He never let anyone touch anything in his room. Even now it was still unmade.

*Maybe Daddy fell asleep on the couch like he sometimes does.*

She went downstairs. The air was cold like the heat had been off too long—her parents turned it down at night to save power.

The living room was empty.

"Dad?" she called softly.

No answer.

She went to the garage. The car was gone.

*He left.*

"Sophie!" Her mother's voice came from behind her. She swooped her up and carried her back inside. "Barefoot in the cold!"

"Where's Dad?" Sophie asked, already knowing. Her mother didn't answer.

"Mom?"

"He'll come back soon."

The light above them flickered, then went out.

"Mom!" Sophie squealed, clutching her arm.

"It's okay. It'll come back in a second."

It did. The generator growled to life.

"See?" Clara said.

"How's Daddy going to come back?"

"He has enough gas, baby."

"But Caleb took one of the canisters," Sophie whispered afraid of her own words, letting her mother fill in the blanks.

Clara looked at her, then away.

"It's going to be okay," she said and kissed Sophie's head— her voice, like her lips, was cold.

The lights flickered again. The generator coughed a wet, hacking sound, like Sophie when she was sick, then died taking the light with it.

# THE END

# ACKNOWLEDGMENTS

Huge thanks to SB Rogue and Charlie Morgan, dear friends and talented authors who helped whip this story into shape.

To my editor, Ayee Caparra of By Moonlight Words Literary Services. You have a gift for turning words into gold. Thank you.

To my mother-in-law, Connie, thank you for taking the time to read and sanity-check my writing.

To Kailey and Lena, for your invaluable help in localizing this story.

And, of course, to my husband, Wes, who supports me in everything I do.

One day, he came to me and said, "I have a book idea for you."

I responded with a long lecture about how an idea is only 0.0000001% of a book—writers never run out of those. It's everything that comes after that makes a book, and that's why you should not approach an author with such things.

Then he told me what he had in mind.

And I loved it.

That's the origin story of *Fairbanks*.

And thank you, dear reader, for supporting this work and for being the final, essential part of this story.

# ABOUT THE AUTHOR

D.G. Woods is a dark fiction author specializing in stories that blur the line between the mundane and the macabre. She is the author of the Appalachian supernatural thriller, **Into the Dark, We Go**, and the dystopian family drama, **Fairbanks**.

Based on the East Coast, Woods describes her work as "just real enough to make you question reality."

She draws her inspiration from the darkest corners of the world, speculating on unsettling "what if" scenarios and the vivid imagery of her own nightmares.

## CONNECT ONLINE

www.dg-woods.com
@pagesnshadows

www.ingramcontent.com/pod-product-compliance
Lightning Source LLC
Chambersburg PA
CBHW050417110726